SWAN SONG IN PUERTO VALLARTA

Brian Emburgh

Note for Librarians: a cataloguing record for this book that includes Dewey Decimal
Classification and US Library of Congress numbers is available from the Library and
Archives of Canada. The complete cataloguing record can be obtained from their online
database at:
www.collectionscanada.ca/amicus/index-e.html
ISBN 1-4120-4193-7
Printed in Victoria, BC, Canada

TRAFFORD

Offices in Canada, USA, Ireland, UK and Spain
This book was published on-demand in cooperation with Trafford Publishing. On-demand
publishing is a unique process and service of making a book available for retail sale to the
public taking advantage of on-demand manufacturing and Internet marketing. On-demand
publishing includes promotions, retail sales, manufacturing, order fulfilment, accounting and
collecting royalties on behalf of the author.
Book sales for North America and international:
Trafford Publishing, 6E–2333 Government St.,
Victoria, BC v8т 4p4 CANADA
phone 250 383 6864 (toll-free 1 888 232 4444)
fax 250 383 6804; email to orders@trafford.com
Book sales in Europe:
Trafford Publishing (uk) Ltd., Enterprise House, Wistaston Road Business Centre,
Wistaston Road, Crewe, Cheshire cw2 7rp UNITED KINGDOM
phone 01270 251 396 (local rate 0845 230 9601)
facsimile 01270 254 983; orders.uk@trafford.com
Order online at:
www.trafford.com/robots/04-2000.html

10 9 8 7

I too am lucky enough to have a black-eyed girl who believes in me. Thanks, Brenda.

Thanks, Melissa for your unconditional love. You are a very special person.

Thanks, Mum and Dad for always being there.

Thanks, Diane for accepting a brother like me.

Some say that a swan sings a beautiful song just before it dies. Maybe, it's not dying. Maybe, it's starting a new life.

The Beginning

After listening to what seemed like the hundredth ring of his bedside telephone, the first laconic words to escape Billy Emmerson's dry, foul-tasting mouth were: "Holy Christ!"

Raising the receiver to his ear with a shaky hand, and steadying it there for perhaps thirty seconds, his next hazy proclamation for the morning was: "Leave me alone, asshole!"

Without waiting for a reply, Billy slammed the receiver down hard into the cradle, pulled the covers over his throbbing head, and hoped like hell that five or six more hours of sleep would alleviate the symptoms of a long night of bad whiskey and fairly decent smoke.

Billy was wrong. After awakening, or more appropriately, coming to, shortly after four, he didn't feel much better at all. A cold beer might help. Maybe a joint would clear his head. After all, he didn't have to be anywhere until seven. Plenty of time to clean up and grab something greasy to line his queasy stomach. *Thank you, God for McDonald's.*

At six fifty-eight, Billy Emmerson emerged from a taxi in front of David Hanson's small bungalow on Cross Street and was met by his second pelting of cold rain of the evening. The first had occurred when he stumbled out of his dreary ground floor apartment twenty minutes earlier. At least his head was beginning to feel attached to his body once more — not screwed on

1

too tightly, but attached.

Before he could reach the porch, the door swung open and Billy was met by the tall, lanky form of the bassist for his group, The Chicago Squires. With his shoulder-length brown hair and delicate features, David Hanson could easily pass for a choir boy with some type of hormonal imbalance. Tonight however, his usual serious countenance was transformed into a caricature of a grinning, agitated, six-foot four scarecrow.

"What's happening?" inquired Billy with feigned interest, as he stepped in out of the rain.

"Didn't Frank tell you?"

"Yeah, but Levinski's losin' it, man. He woke me up around ten trying to be funny. I didn't laugh."

With uncharacteristic good humour, David replied: "Come here. I want to show you something."

Soon, Billy and David found themselves settled around the familiar old, stained and cigarette burned blue Formica table in David's kitchen. After a moment of silence, while staring at David's still grinning face, Billy felt his curiosity beginning to peek. David was trying to tell him something, but, he didn't quite know how. Broaching the silence with what seemed like a logical and timely question, Billy asked, "Where's everybody else? I thought we were supposed to practice for next month."

"Not tonight, man. They've all gone home or are out partying!" David took a deep breath and continued. "Just listen for a second, okay? When Frank cut the deal with that shitty little record company a few months ago, nobody, not even me, thought the album would sell a dozen copies. Seems like it sold a few more."

With that assertion, Billy Emmerson's bassist and writing partner reached over to the cluttered kitchen counter and carefully retrieved an open copy of the current Billboard Magazine, placing it in front of the skeptical guitar player's face. "Look at the fuckin' chart, Billy!"

For the second time that day, the only fitting declaration Billy could utter was, "Holy Christ!"

"Hard Driven Rain" peaked at number three on May 7, 1982 and, for the next several months, life was very good for The Chicago Squires.

Frank Levinski, The Squires' manager, and the least likely to become affected by the entire experience, seemed to metamorphose on an almost daily basis. Levinski, short, stocky, prematurely balding, and inclined to smoke cheap cigars, began to rule the group with an iron hand. Always tight with a dime, he now became a tyrant about socking away every cent the band made. The only concession Frank made to his new found wealth was a penchant for devouring rich cream éclairs at every given opportunity. On several occasions, the band members smirked as tiny globs of cream dripped from the corners of his mouth as he berated one of the musicians for some unnecessary expenditure. Perhaps Frank knew something or had some half-buried premonition. Even an animal will store fat for the lean times ahead.

David Hanson handled his good fortune professionally, but with a great sense of immediacy.

Sure, he enjoyed the bigger gigs, the groupies, the money, and all the other perks his newly found success afforded him, but, with it all, came a sense of urgency. David wanted to hang on to what he now possessed.

Luckily, for The Chicago Squires, he had

become the glue that held the band together at this point. Though resolute, David retained a dry sense of humor, and a smile would still break upon his rigid and sombre countenance on a sporadic basis. He was the one who forced the group to practice when everyone else wanted to kick back and enjoy the life of minor rock stars. He was the one who had to coerce Billy into sitting down with a six string acoustic guitar in order to write. David's lyrics were good, and his music more than adequate, but without the spark of creativity Billy seemed to possess innately, the bassist's own tunes never seemed to ascend to the exceptional level.

Unlike Frank or David however, Billy Emmerson drank in the new life with unbridled passion and excess. His thirst was unquenchable. Never having had much as a kid growing up in the "bad" side of the city, Billy intended to make up for lost time.

Instead of the traditional T-shirt and jeans, he now chose to squeeze his six-foot body into tight leather pants and form-fitting shirts. *Just like a young Elvis!* he imagined.

Other changes were made. Billy, with some reluctance, decided to have his long mane of unruly dirty-blonde hair trimmed and his beard of three years scraped away. After the shearing, while staring into the mirror of the pricey salon, his gaze was met by that of a young man with pale blue eyes and handsome features. Slowly a grin, or perhaps something more akin to a leer, appeared on his newly discovered face. *I'm gonna like this fuckin' gig,* he thought.

For the next several months, Billy's life became a blur. Sometimes days would slip by and he couldn't remember how he had filled them. One party seemed to flow into the next, except that with each successful concert, the grass became sweeter and the labels on the wine bottles were now printed in French.

He still got together with the rest of the group for requisite rehearsals, but Billy couldn't see much point in it. They knew the songs inside out. Besides, Billy had other things to do.

The young guitarist had always liked and respected Jake Andrews, the drummer and, Toby Tap, the band's keyboard player: indispensable spokes on the spinning wheel. Like Billy, they too were enjoying the ride but, occasionally, stepped off the carousel to regain their balance.

Lately however, Billy's patience with everyone seemed stretched. He had no use for small talk before practices and he could care less about some tour their manager was always yapping about. Everything was cool just the way it was.

He and David still went through the motions of writing, but, although he didn't realize it, Billy's songs were becoming contrite and almost predictable in their structures and outcomes. After one night of futile collaboration, an almost imperceptible shadow of doubt crept into David's voice. "What's the matter, man?"

"Nothing, really, I'm just tired I guess."

"If I lived like you, I'd be tired too! Do you think we're going to be ready on time for the second album? Frank says we have to be in the studio in two weeks."

"Yeah, sure," replied Billy. "Everything's golden. Just relax a little, Davey, my boy."

"You think the songs are okay?"

"As good as they're ever gonna get," muttered Billy.

His own irony was wasted.

Oh, Sweet Lizzy

Three months later, Billy awoke around eleven to the sounds of dishes rattling and the tea kettle shrieking.

"What the hell are you doing, Lizzy?" he called from the bedroom.

Lizzy Blair was a beautiful twenty-year old nymphette whom Billy had met six weeks earlier while playing a concert in Detroit. She was dumber than a fence post, but had the longest legs and firmest butt Billy had ever seen.

"I'm making you breakfast, Baby!" she responded in a loud nasal voice from the kitchen.

"I'm really not hungry right now." *Christ, she has a whiney voice,* thought Billy.

"But, Baby..."

"Not now, Lizzy! I'm still waking up!"

Billy hated it when she called him, "Baby." He was also beginning to tire of their live-in arrangement despite the never-ending bouts of carnal bliss. Billy was beginning to tire of everything lately.

"Baby, Frank called 'bout twenty minutes ago. Said it was important."

"Yeah, okay, I'm gonna see him tonight anyway." *Shit!* Billy thought, *I wish she wouldn't call me that.*

With that, he rolled over, pulled the sheets over his head in order to drown out the domestic banging still emanating from the kitchen, and fell into the land of rock 'n' roll dreams.

All Things Must Pass
(Eventually)

By eight that night, everyone had gathered around the comfortable table in David's kitchen waiting for Frank to arrive.

Anticipating good news concerning the second album gave the gathering a certain festive quality which was heightened further when David ceremoniously brought forth a bottle of Jack Daniel's and Jake withdrew a fat joint from his inner vest pocket.

"Sure is hard to believe that eight months ago we were playing hotels for rent and beer money," stated Toby philosophically.

"Yeah, but eight months ago, I didn't have to listen to Lizzy's voice every waking moment!" Billy moaned.

Sympathetic laughter was cut short by a steady authoritative burst of knocking on David's front door. The bass player arose to answer the summons, and, seconds later, Frank Levinski had seated himself between Billy and David at the conference table.

Frank, because of his long-running love affair with rich desserts, had gained considerable bulk over the months. He now resembled a penguin wearing a T-shirt proclaiming: "John Lennon Died for Our Sins!" The buckle of his pants had stretched to the end of its line and the flap covering the zipper was beginning to pull away from its intended position.

There was nothing comical in Frank's face tonight, however.

Accepting a glass of J.D., he stared solemnly at the scarred table, not knowing where to start or how to avoid what had to be said.

"What's happening, man?" inquired David.

"This is what's happening," began Frank slowly and choosing his words carefully. "I just got back from a meeting with the producers. The new album hasn't quite broken into the top ten yet. In fact, they don't even think it will ever appear on the top million. Said the songs are crap and not a jockey in the city will waste his time giving them any air play. Not only that, but, the gig next Saturday has to be cancelled — not enough tickets sold."

The party broke up early that night.

Somewhere Between a Rock 'n' a Roll

For Billy Emmerson, the new year rang in with a dull thud.

With each passing day, it seemed as if some personal clock buried deep within his mind were being pushed backward by a crazed cuckoo or a pair of insane woodcutters sawing for eternity on a plastic log.

In some respects, Billy had begun to slip back slowly and imperceptibly into his old life. Gone were the leathers, flashy jewellery, and the constant swirl of mind numbing parties.

In other ways, he began to acquire traits he never knew he possessed. He stoically came to terms with the fact that in all probability, The Chicago Squires would never have another hit record. They would remain, at best, a decent little four-piece combo working for decent little wages in decent little bars.

Billy's brash cockiness and smug bravado had subsided considerably. After all, what was left to fuel his inflated ego?

The band still made fairly good money riding on the popularity of "Hard Driven Rain," and the royalty cheques still trickled in, but Billy soon realized that the audiences were becoming smaller with each successive hotel or dingy arena in which they played . Sometimes, Billy would work his ass off, but nobody seemed to be listening.

He still enjoyed getting together with David

and considered him a good friend. There were even rare occasions when the two thought they had written something good. Those times were becoming fewer and further apart however.

Frank Levinski had gained a growing respect in Billy's eyes. Levinski's loyalty to the band and blunt honesty were characteristics that the guitar player had come to admire.

For the most part, playing with The Squires was still fun, but there were times when singing the "old" tunes was almost an embarrassment.

On one occasion, just before the opening set at some dimly lit downtown club, Billy overheard a pimply-faced kid, trying to impress his underage girlfriend, comment, with all the coolness he could muster: "These guys aren't too bad. They even had a record out a little while ago."

It was not one of Billy's best performances that night.

On the other hand, Lizzy would not be there when he returned home. She had left as soon as the pay cheques had begun to dwindle in size and frequency.

Vague Plans Begin to Formulate

A little over a year after the success of "Hard Driven Rain," a nebulous notion began to creep into Billy's thoughts with increasing frequency. At first, the idea stole into his mind slowly, like fog rolling over Chicago's damp, grey pavement on a chilly morning.

Maybe it was the recent abstinence from grass and booze. Rather than mellowing him out, the old vices now tended to put Billy in a morose frame of mind. He didn't need that. Billy, for the first time in his life, was beginning to think of the future.

Perhaps the fog was lifting.

A Decision

Billy had called a meeting with Frank and David. Four hours later, the three found themselves once more situated around David's dilapidated kitchen table.

David was the first to speak. "What's goin' on, Billy? Got some plans for a big tour?"

"No, not really," replied Billy, forcing himself to smile, "but I have to talk to you guys about something."

Frank remained silent.

Billy continued. "I don't want to do this anymore. It's no good. The whole thing was great for awhile, but now it's over. Maybe it's just me. If I fucked up, I'm sorry. You guys are my friends and I owe you, but I want out."

It was David's turn to keep quiet.

Frank spoke next. "Look, Billy, we made some money, had a good time. The royalty cheques still come in once in awhile. We can still do alright."

"No. It's not what I want, Frank. I want to get out of this city and start again."

"Where will you go?" asked David, with no attempt to hide the anxiety in his voice.

"I don't know. Maybe someplace warm. I think I'd like that."

The three talked for hours about the good times they had shared. There was no animosity concerning Billy's decision. They all realized it couldn't last forever. By the end of the night, they parted with handshakes and promises to always keep in touch.

Independence Day
July 4, 1983.

Billy awoke early feeling fresh and alert.

He was pleased with his new surroundings, and pleased with the tranquillity they had helped him achieve.

As the kettle began to whistle, Billy gazed out of his kitchen window onto Calle 31 de Octubre. The sun had not yet climbed over the hills to the east, but he could clearly discern the silhouette of the solitary, gnarled tamarind tree defining his side of the cobblestone boulevard.

Soon, ancient blue and white buses would be rumbling along Ordaz, a few blocks to the west, and people would languidly swing open doors and set out on their daily routines.

Nothing moved too quickly here, except perhaps, the dusty yellow taxi cabs. T-shirts, which tourists seemed to purchase by the gross, encapsulated the town's philosophy precisely: "Mañana, I'm on Mexican time!" Tomorrow would be time enough.

As Billy finished his second cup of strong, black *café clásico*, he wondered where the streets might lead him today. The sun was now up, and the day promised to be a duplicate of the one before — hot, sunny and filled with the scent of sub-tropical flowers for which Billy knew no name.

Although the tourist brochures typically proclaimed Puerto Vallarta as a "sleepy little fishing village located on the shore of Bandaras Bay," Billy knew otherwise. After walking for hours each day, his drained muscles told him the town was far more encompassing than first imagined.

Billy was constantly amazed at the subtle nuances of colour and texture the town offered up to him.

Most buildings and homes were painted or washed in brilliant white, and pastel shades of blue, pink or green often framed doorways and windows. Overlapping, trough-shaped terra-cotta tiles covered sun baked roofs. Black, twisted wrought-iron enclosed the numerous balconies upon which brightly painted pots of intricate design contained cacti or plants blooming with flame red flowers.

Trees and shrubs abounded everywhere. Tall palms, bearing coconuts or up-turned bananas, seemed to reach higher on a daily basis in their quest for sun. Hibiscus and benjaminas were pruned by machete lest they grew too ungainly. Delicate bougainvilleas cascaded over balconies or rooftops, stopping just short of the sidewalks below.

In The Centro, or Old Vallarta area in which Billy lived, all of the streets were lined in cobblestones hauled from the beaches of Bandaras Bay. The steady beat of iron-shod horses, or donkeys drawing carts as they traversed these avenues, reminded Billy of some long-forgotten rhythm The Squires were never quite able to capture.

Although the young man from the "Windy City" had no particular place to be today, he felt comfortable and relaxed adhering to his daily regimen of exploration. The sights and sounds of the city were more intoxicating than any stimulus he had ever inhaled or ingested.

Time to be off.

Time to begin.

Stepping tentatively down the cobblestone grade from his second story apartment, Billy soon crossed Ordaz.

Locating his favorite boulder on the breakwall of the Hotel Rosita, Billy could now hunch down comfortably. From here, he was able to observe the fishermen, a stone's throw to the south, as they hauled in their catches to the open air market between the beach and Ordaz.

The market was a popular place for locals to purchase fresh fish and for tourists to pose for their cameras. Captions scrawled on the back of photographs proclaiming, "Look what Dad caught for supper!" were always in vogue.

Fat pelicans were welcome partners and treated kindly by the fishermen. They were allowed to perch on the crude wooden boats, and tolerated, as they eagerly snatched up anything escaping through the nets as they were dragged aboard. As entrails were discarded onto the beach after cleaning at the market, dozens of the greedy fowl would stagger to the feast like drunken sailors at a free buffet. Symbiosis in the sand.

Billy was enthralled with the dexterity with which nets were mended by what appeared to be the elders of this small community of *pescadors*. Lean brown fingers with blackened nails would nimbly repair gashes with no apparent effort. Where there had been a tear, these wrinkled magicians would employ a wooden needle the size of a steak knife to suture the wound as skillfully as any trained surgeon.

The sun had begun to rise higher in the sky and Billy could feel droplets of sweat forming on his forehead. His shoulders were beginning to burn.

As a concession to the heat, Billy, as of late, had taken to wearing light cotton undershirts and high-cut shorts tailored from a pair of old blue jeans upon which he had operated. His running shoes were still holding out, although dust and street grime were beginning to stain them a dingy grey.

Out of necessity, the guitar player had procured his first Mexican haircut two weeks ago. This time, his rock 'n' roll tresses were snipped to within an inch or two by a smiling, middle-aged señora with a flare for employing hair clips to measure the precise length of locks to be removed. Although the sign above the low, swinging saloon-style doors read "Unisex," Billy felt slightly embarrassed when tourists strolled by, gawked and smiled at the only man in the establishment sporting pink plastic clips in his hair. *Hell,* Billy thought at the time, *at least I'll be cooler!*

The sun was now directly overhead and it was time to move on.

"It's hard work doing nothing," Billy uttered to himself.

Retracing his steps back across Ordaz, Billy made a quick stop at the corner store where he was greeted by Paco, the owner, with a familiar, "Hola, amigo!"

"Hola," responded Billy. *"Cómo está ?"*

"Good, my friend! Time for a beer?"

"Sounds good, Paco! It's hot out there!"

Although the American had begun to pick up a smattering of Spanish words and expressions, he was always thankful that most of the residents were conversant with some English.

Sliding open the glass door of the cooler, Billy withdrew a frosty can of Modelo and popped the tab before paying for it. *Breakfast of Champions!* thought the thirsty rambler.

Reimbursing Paco at the counter, and departing with an *"Hasta luego!"* Billy stepped out onto the sidewalk and contemplated in which direction he would now roam.

Rather than crossing over to the Malecón, the wide "boardwalk" separating the ocean from the street, where beer drinking was frowned upon by the local police, he decided to stick to the still shady side of the sidewalk on Ordaz and make his way southward.

The shops and restaurants were now engaged

in brisk business and, on every corner, attractive young Mexicans could be seen and heard delivering well rehearsed pitches in the hopes of luring gullible tourists into purchasing time shares with promises of free breakfasts, cheap rates and complimentary Jeep usage for a week. Billy was immune. By this time, his face was familiar and smiles and pleasantries were all that were expected or required.

Continuing south, Billy was pleased when he noticed the doors of one particular *farmacia* or drugstore were swung open and the pretty young señorita at whom he had smiled on numerous occasions was visible behind the counter. She was busily engaged in selling sunscreen to a pair of tourists suffering with blazing, neon pink complexions. *One of these days, I'm gonna ask her her name,* thought Billy. Perhaps now wasn't the best time though. Well-done lobsters took precedent.

The trek continued.

Drifting slowly, in accordance with the heat of the day and his own indolent mood, Billy Emmerson arrived at the two lane bridge spanning the shallow Rio Cuale. Often he would lean against the concrete sides of the crossing and crane his neck while trying to spot iguanas or long-legged birds on either bank.

Today, however, he decided to spend a leisurely sojourn on the island below the bridge. A community unto itself, the *isla* supported shops, museums and several fine restaurants.

A smile crossed the face of Vallarta's vernal vagabond as he descended the dozen or so steps leading from the bridge to the bustle below. He was familiar by this time with most of the island's vendors and enjoyed the good-hearted banter and animated sales pitches each delivered to curious passersby.

Treading by each successive shop, Billy was greeted by typical inquiries. He responded with typical aloofness.

"Hola, amigo! Want to buy some T-shirts? Almost free today!"

"No, gracias. Already have one."

"Silver for your wife or secretary, my friend?"

"No, don't have either. Thanks though."

"Onyx chess set? Half price!"

"Don't know how to play."

"Sandals? Good price for you!"

"Running shoes still okay, amigo."

"How 'bout a blanket, señor?"

"Maybe next time. It's too hot today."

And so it went. It was fun.

After exploring the shops and exchanging quips with the island's entrepreneurs for the better part of the afternoon, Billy decided it was time to depart. His rumbling stomach told him a cheeseburger or two might be in order.

As with most young men however, the hint of romance often overpowered such base human longings as hunger. Billy was no exception.

A short walk north, soon found the young street-comber quickening his pace as he neared the drugstore on Ordaz, which he had passed several hours earlier.

Billy thought: *I suppose now is as good a time as any to ask her what her name is.* As he approached the store, he wiped his brow with the back of his hand. He took a few more tentative paces. He stepped through the entrance way.

She wasn't there.

In her place, behind the counter, stood a taller, slightly older version of the girl he had seen working earlier in the day. Around her neck, she wore a gold chain with a pendant engraved with her name. It was "Patti."

Her easy smile quickly disarmed Billy. He felt awkward and slightly embarrassed. He hoped his stomach wouldn't make noises.

"I...umm...Do you have any...gum?" murmured Billy.

"Si . It's right in front of you," answered Patti in an openly playful tone.

Selecting the nearest package, Billy withdrew a collection of coins from his pocket and held the pesos out to Patti in his open palm. Counting in Spanish, the saleslady slowly picked out the appropriate change and thanked Billy for his purchase. Once again, she smiled.

Billy returned her smile and boldly decided to make another inquiry. "Señorita, do you know the girl who was working here this morning?"

"Si. Yes, I do. It was my sister, Raquel. You must be Billy."

"How do you know that?"

"We asked around."

Feeling his face growing flushed, Billy turned with all the cool he could muster, smiled again at the pretty señorita, and made his way out of the small *farmacia*.

Jesus, he thought, *what will I do now?*

Making his way to Paco's didn't take long. Billy entered with a grin pasted upon his tanned face.

"What's happening, amigo? *Qué pasa?*" inquired the proprietor.

"Not much," answered Billy "but I think I'm in love!"

"Who's the lucky señorita?" asked the storekeeper.

"That's just it. It could be with two señoritas!" answered Billy.

It was now Paco's turn to grin. "Sounds like you could use a beer."

"No," responded a befuddled Mr. Emmerson, "I think I'll take a six-pack."

Carrying his purchase in a plastic bag, Billy crossed Jésus Langarica, climbed a few concrete steps, and soon found himself seated upon a white, wrought-iron bench facing Parque Hidalgo.

With his back turned toward the bustling Avenido México, the city's newest son could observe the nightly routines of the park with amusement and unwavering fascination. Since the onset of his arrival, Billy had always enjoyed this particular sector of the Old Town and had looked forward to basking in its circus-like atmosphere on a regular basis.

A warm glow from several ancient street lights scattered throughout the park was beginning to illuminate islands of sub-tropical trees and shrubs situated on each side of wide concrete walkways. Peering upward, through the fronds of a tall palm, Billy easily imagined that each iron-winged gargoyle, perched above the three white orbs on each street lamp, was guarding its own minuscule territory in Hidalgo.

Vendors and enterprising minor restauranteurs were busily preparing for the evening in anticipation of a brisk tourist trade. Each such person of commerce was responsible for wheeling his or her large cart, from the storage area at the back of the park, into its designated reserved space. Worn extension cords had to be carefully spliced into the partially open base of twisted wires on each park light. Bulbs had to be strung along the front of canvas awnings covering most of the mobile places of business.

Lights were beginning to flicker on from many of the small establishments lending a festive atmosphere to the entire park.

Tourists and local people alike were beginning to flood the walkway in front of Billy.

The smells of crêpes, frying strips of succulent pork and onions, and the pungent odor of Mexican spices brought Mr. Emmerson back to the realization that he hadn't yet eaten. Still time for one more beer though.

Rising from his bench, carrying a *cerveza* in one hand and a bag containing the remaining two cans in the other, Billy decided to stretch his legs and visit a newly acquired acquaintance who was situated at the end of Hidalgo facing Calle Venezuela. "Bruno" was the title Billy had bestowed upon the vendor after finding his real name unpronounceable. Bruno seemed to think his redubbing a wonderful gift and always laughed good-naturedly when greeted by Billy.

"Hola, Bruno! How's business?"

"Good, Billy. I think tonight I sell a lot of junk! Make lots of money. Go to America. Buy a pink Cadillac. Live in Hollywood!"

"Well, Bruno, maybe tonight's the night," replied Billy with mock seriousness. "Care for a *cerveza*, amigo?"

"No, gracias, Billy. I am working much too hard now."

Well, thought Billy, draining his fourth can, *you'll have to work a hell of a lot harder to buy a Caddy and live in California!*

Bruno sold ceramic necklaces, pens, ash trays, coffee mugs and cheap T-shirts. He would never be rich, but always appeared jovial and content with his allotted place in Parque Hidalgo.

"Gotta get going, buddy," uttered Billy, snapping the tab of another beer. "It's been a long day and I'm hungry."

"Okay, amigo. Maybe see you tomorrow," Bruno responded with a smile and a wave of his hand.

Wobbling slightly, Billy wound his way through the ever increasing crowd back to his bench. Amazingly, it was still empty.

Within seconds of snapping open his last beer, he glanced up to see his friend, Hermano approaching from his own souvenir stand about twenty feet away.

Hermano was a short, paunchy vendor who sported a neatly-trimmed, thin mustache. He seemed to be in a constant state of motion. Although he always employed one or two people to help him hawk his gaudy trinkets, if Hermano strayed from the store for any length of time, he would grow agitated and restless. Even in the middle of a conversation, he would steal furtive glances back toward his stand to reassure himself that all was well. When, at last, the chubby proprietor felt compelled that he must touch base, he would raise a finger to a spot below his right cheekbone and assert: "Business!" Off he would be to mind his establishment.

"Hola, Billy!" cried Hermano as he neared. "What's happening, amigo?"

"Nothing, *nada*," answered Billy as the two shook hands. "I was just thinking of getting something to eat. Wanna join me?"

"Maybe later," replied Hermano with a wide smile. "Now, I feel like the celebration! I finally sell that much ugly mask to honeymooners from New York for five-hundred pesos! Told them it was the Aztec god of Fertility."

"Congratulations!" exclaimed Billy, while

shaking hands once again. "You're one smart *hombre!*"

"Gracias," answered Hermano with pride in his voice. "Maybe I am! Come, we will buy the tequila!"

"I don't know, Hermano. It's been a long time since I touched any of that stuff." The six cans of beer that Billy had just consumed however, broke down his resolve almost immediately. "Hell, why not, amigo? Maybe a little wouldn't hurt."

With that decision made, the two friends set off through the park and across Langarica to Paco's to purchase their powerful Mexican elixir.

Billy wavered ever so slightly. Twice he stumbled on cobblestones while crossing the street. Hermano walked with a swagger; Billy, with a stagger.

After obtaining their bottle from a young man employed by Paco, Hermano thought it might be a prudent idea to return to the souvenir stand in order to imbibe at their leisure, while, at the same time, taking care of business. They could also watch tall American señoritas stroll by. Billy readily agreed to the plan and soon the two found themselves back at the shop sipping tequila from coffee cups depicting paradise in Puerto Vallarta.

After an hour had passed, and the better part of their bottle had been killed, Billy decided to confide in Hermano about the two beautiful women working at the *farmacia* on Ordaz.

"I'll tell you somethin', Hermano. I bet if we

finish this ol' bottle of ours really pronto, and get movin' now, those two might still be there. Wanna go for a walk?"

"Sounds good, amigo. I love the beautiful ladies!"

After Hermano had informed a young employee of his future whereabouts, the pair gingerly navigated Langarica once again. What should have been a few minutes leisurely walk, turned into an obstacle course which tested their ambulatory skills with every step. Every curb became a challenge and every tourist seemed to intentionally block their passage. Finally, they arrived at the drugstore.

"Jus' let me do the talkin' ol' boy! They already know me," slurred Billy as the two conspired before entering.

"Okay, my friend. I trust you, but my heart goes beating already!" responded Hermano while trying to steady himself.

Stepping inside with a great attempt at sobriety, Billy and Hermano discerned an elderly gentleman with a shiny bald head and reading glasses perched upon a long hawk-like nose. Exchanging glances of disappointment, the two shrugged, but decided to proceed to the counter and make inquiries anyway. They hadn't come this far for nothing.

"Buenos noches, señor. Do you happen to know where the two girls are who were workin' here this afternoon might be, sir?" inquired Billy hopefully.

"No hablo English, señor," stated the clerk apologetically.

"Is no problem, Billy," whispered Hermano to his cohort. "I find out everything about this matter."

The conversation between Hermano and the pharmacist ensued too rapidly for Billy to comprehend much of it, but in the end, an obviously pleased Hermano faced Billy, touched the place below his right eye, winked, nodded and smiled broadly.

"All is well, amigo! They are both in the back changing the clothing. They must know the great lovers are here for them!" announced Hermano with lewd delight. "The manager goes to inform them of our arrival."

"Good work, my man! Now get ready to meet two of Vallarta's most beautiful women!" exclaimed the elated match-maker.

As if on cue, the door at the back of the *farmacia* swung open and two young señoritas appeared, grinning bashfully. They were not however, Patti and Raquel.

"*Beautiful*" was not the first adjective which sprang to Billy's mind when viewing them for the first time. Both were dressed in blue jeans which did nothing to flatter their short, but more than ample figures. Both wore crisp white blouses which strained to the point where buttons would burst if either gained another ounce around her bosom.

The taller of the two, by perhaps an inch, had a smile that even in his present condition, Billy would never forget. Surrounding each large front tooth, was a band of glistening silver apparently applied by a demented dentist for reasons completely beyond Billy's comprehension.

The second young lady chose to wear her hair in thick, luxuriant braids, each culminating in a stretched elastic — one red, the other purple. It was readily apparent, that through the arm holes of her sleeveless blouse, this shorter señorita also sported enough thatch to warrant the use of several more elastics.

Thank God she's wearing jeans, thought Billy, *I'd hate to see her legs!*

Turning to his partner, with a look that begged forgiveness, Billy spoke softly enough for only his friend to hear: "Sorry, amigo. I've never seen these two in my life! I'm gonna think of some way to get outta this mess."

"Are you *loco*? They're beautiful!" exclaimed Hermano with lustful enthusiasm. "I must only ask if I might escort the tall one."

"What the hell," philosophized Mr. Emmerson, through a tequila haze, "we've gone this far!"

"Okay, I make everything good. Just follow along and it will be the most best night!"

With that drunken boast, Hermano approached the two señoritas, and, speaking in Spanish, introduced himself, explained the error his American friend had made in mistaken identities, and asked the ladies if they would care to partake in dinner despite the unworthiness of two such foolish companions.

31

My Kingdom for an Aspirin

Billy awoke the next day at around twelve with very little recollection of what had transpired the previous evening. Vague images of dinner, stumbling along the Malecón, and drinking beer in some little dive flashed into his brain when he tried to concentrate. As far as any romantic liaison having occurred, Billy was *relatively* certain there had been none.

Hermano's evening however may have ended quite differently.

Soaking in Paradise

It was now November and Billy's life had fallen into a pattern of idyllic existence.

The young musician continued to roam the streets with a never-ending sense of adventure and awe. Each day would yield new treasures to absorb, behold, and savour. Sometimes he would discover an unexplored side street where shallow bins of shrimp, red snapper and fresh squid resting on beds of crushed ice had been set up to serve as a makeshift open air market. Often, if Billy returned the next day to make a purchase, he found the temporary market had disappeared to a new location waiting to be discovered.

Occasionally, the explorer would ascend one of the many dirt paths leading up into the verdant mountains east of the city. Huts constructed of discarded or "found" bits of lumber and corrugated sheet metal dotted the elevated landscape at regular intervals. Each shelter, and surrounding claimed pieces of jungle, characteristically housed two or three adults, several children, scrawny yelping dogs, diminutive brightly plumed fowl and, nimble foraging pigs. Since no electricity existed in this remote altitude, it was always a puzzle to Billy how cold beer could be purchased from a family member for one American dollar.

Beach combing also held a fascination for Vallarta's new convert. Billy preferred to stick closely to the shoreline of Bandaras Bay where he could successfully scavenge shells, polished glass and pieces of driftwood to decorate his small apartment. If he strayed too closely to the meticulously raked beaches near the hotels, he would find himself tripping over bodies of well-oiled tourists or dodging volleyballs driven by teenagers testing their libidos in the sun.

Billy also enjoyed the white-clad pedlars who flocked to the tourists in hopes of selling them authentic Mexican keepsakes and one-of-a-kind items, but how many ceramic *burros* did one person need?

It was good to be breathing. Edification in Eden.

Levinski's Letter

You'd better get to work, my boy,
And earn some spending pay,
'Cause without some folding money,
You can't buy the time of day.

- Jumpin' Joanne and the Dunks, 1977

In early April of 1984, Billy Emmerson was
surprised to receive a letter from Chicago,
Illinois, U.S.A. It was from Frank Levinski.
Although Billy had sent Frank his address
several months ago when the musician had
settled in Vallarta, this was the first personal
correspondence to arrive. All others had been
undersized royalty payments from "Hard Driven
Rain" sales.
  The letter was terse:

Dear Billy,
  *Hope everything is good on the beach. What
are the women like? We're doing okay up here,
but I'm sure the weather isn't as good.*
  *I lost three pounds and am starting to look like
a freakin' movie star! Ha! Ha! Have you ever
thought about coming home? The cheques have
stopped.*
  Maybe we could get the band back together.
                              Take care,
                              Frank

Well, thought Billy, *it's not like I didn't know*

35

this would happen. Shit!

The problem facing the ex-Squire however, was that he had no intention of leaving his new home despite his financial situation. He was happier here than at any other time in his life. He felt as if he were part of something. He felt he belonged.

Billy calculated his savings would sustain life for another couple of months, but once they were depleted, a steady source of income was an unequivocal requirement.

Time to Think

The next morning, Billy arose, as usual, with the morning sun. His apartment on "Hallowe'en Street" was becoming the first real home the American musician had ever felt was a part of his own personality and evolving lifestyle.

Colorful water colors depicting lively street scenes, the Church of Guadalupé, and fishing boats riding the waters of Bandaras Bay adorned the once barren chalky walls of the living area. Striped blankets of kaleidoscope tones hung loosely over stark cracked leather and lattice furniture. Even Billy's cramped kitchen, with its gas stove and ancient refrigerator, seemed more personal with the acquisition of three small potted cacti thriving on the narrow window sill.

Mulling over the question of shrinking finances over his second cup of strong Mexican coffee, Billy decided to forgo his daily regimen of town combing for a slow ascent into the lush mountainous jungle. In the tranquil solitude of the thick sub-tropical foliage, he would be able to think clearly and uninterrupted.

Setting out at just past nine, he climbed steadily for three hours until he reached the destination he knew would be conducive to pondering his current perturbation.

A narrow meandering stream shaded by sprawling trees afforded Billy a welcome retreat from the intense heat. An outcropping of tumbled pink, grey and ebony river rocks provided a natural seat upon which he could rest his tired muscles.

Immersing himself in this arboreal setting, Billy allowed his mind to drift freely. An hour later, he awoke from a deep, unexpected nap with a smile on his face.

Time to be moving on.

How About It, Hermano?

That evening, after purchasing six cans of cold Modelo from Paco's convenience store, Billy crossed over to Parque Hidalgo from Langarica, claimed his favorite bench, and began the waiting game. As dusk drew near, it was only a matter of time before Hermano would make an appearance. After all, business was business.

Snapping the tab of the first beer of the evening and sipping the cold liquid amber helped put him in a contemplative, yet resolute mood. Watching the locals and tourists parade by, as lights began to flicker and pungent aromas assailed his sense of olfaction, made Billy realize why he had come to love this town so much. People were real and life was simple. This is what he had been searching for all of his life. He was not about to lose his dream.

Billy's musing was cut short as a grinning, cherubic Hermano approached from the general vicinity of his souvenir stand.

"Hey, Hermano! How's business?" inquired Billy as he extended his hand to his friend.

"Very good!" divulged the vendor in an excited tone. "I could be thinking of hiring another assistant soon for the times like this!"

"You don't know how good that is to hear, friend," replied Billy openly. "Sit down. Let's have some *cerveza!* I have a business proposition for you."

The word "business" was all that was required to spark Hermano's curiosity. "What do you think about, Billy?" inquired Hermano as he accepted a can of cold beer.

"Well," began Billy, choosing his words carefully, "like you say, business here seems very good. Most nights, you're making out like a bandido putting in overtime."

"Si," confirmed Hermano, glancing at his bustling stand, touching the traditional spot below his right eye, and smiling broadly.

"I bet that you've been so busy that you don't even have enough time to see that girl from the *farmacia*. She is very beautiful!" The last few words stuck in Billy's throat, but he managed to get them out with exaggerated sincerity.

"Angelica! Yes, she is *muy bonita*. I would want to see her more times because my heart is full." To accentuate his point, Hermano slowly placed the palm of his right hand over his heart and sighed deeply. "She is my angel."

"You know, amigo, I think I can help you out with your problem."

"How can this be?"

"Well, I'm here just about every night anyway, and, it seems to me, that you could use some time off."

Hermano's "Si" seemed to stretch into four syllables.

"Basically, what I'm saying," continued Billy, "is that I could use a job. I don't need much to live on. Food and rent are cheap but, my savings are getting a bit thin."

"Billy, you too are an angel!" exclaimed Hermano, glancing skyward as if to thank the heavenly host. "When can you begin the work?"

"Let's drink some beer tonight! If you like, I can start *mañana*."

"Yes! Tomorrow is good!" agreed Hermano enthusiastically, as the two once again shook hands. "First though, let us check on the business."

As the partners arose from the bench, Billy found himself involuntarily touching a spot under his right eye.

The Musician Gets a Real Job

The next night, as the last rays of sunshine filtered through the palms on the Malecón, Billy met his new employer as he stepped jauntily from his place of business to greet his young friend.

"Hola, Billy! *Cómo está?*"

"I'm fine," answered Billy, as they shook. "How 'bout you? You look very sharp tonight, amigo. What's the occasion?"

"Tonight, I take Angelica for the dinner," replied Hermano, smiling impishly. "Come, my friend. I will inform you of the instructions."

As the pair approached the cart, it was apparent that preparations had already begun for a busy night. Lights had been strung along the stand's canvas awning, coffee cups, ash trays and primitively painted plates had been carefully dusted, and ceramic necklaces and silver plated rings had been meticulously arranged on suspended twine or felt-lined display cases. Hermano's young employee had performed an admirable job.

"Billy, this is my assistant," proclaimed Hermano with profound dignity, as the two stood directly in front of the stand. "He speaks very little of the English, but he is the good worker and he is to be trusted."

"Assistant" appeared to be about fifteen years of age. He was short and thin with carefully coiffed medium-length dark brown hair. The sparse beginnings of a mustache appeared on his upper lip.

As Assistant smiled and reached out to shake Billy's hand, Billy was struck by his uncanny resemblance to Hermano.

No, thought Billy, *I'm not even going to ask.*

"Now," interjected Hermano, "this is how the running of the business works..."

Several minutes later, Billy found himself relieved to learn that his responsibilities would be minimal. Although his Spanish was improving daily, Billy was not yet ready to deal with the Mexican public. He would peddle Hermano's goods to tourists, translate dollars into pesos for them and keep a running inventory of what he had sold each night. Hermano had carefully explained the price of each article to Billy, but in case of the employer's absence, Assistant was there to help. At the end of each shift, Hermano would appear from destinations unknown with his sputtering old pickup, park the truck on Avenido México, and the three would carefully pack the merchandise onto the truck's bed. Hermano would ceremoniously place the cashbox near him on the passenger side and disappear into the night. Billy and Assistant were then left with the task of wheeling the portable emporium back to its assigned designation at the far end of the park. It sounded simple.

"Well, Billy, do you think you will be alright tonight?" questioned Hermano while smiling coyly and smoothing his mustache. "Angelica is probably hungry for the dinner and for me also!

I hope."

"We'll be okay, boss," replied the new employee. "You go ahead and have a good time. Don't worry about a thing."

"Good!" exclaimed Hermano. "I will be off then. *Hasta luego amigos!*"

"*Hosta luego!*" responded Billy and Assistant in unison.

Hermano took perhaps a dozen paces toward Langarica, turned, nodded at his employees, touched his cheek, pivoted, and resumed his quest for romance.

As Hermano blended into the crowd, Billy could not help but notice the fondness and admiration in Assistant's eyes as he followed his employer's every step. "*No,*" thought Billy, "*it's none of my business!*"

Since several potential customers were beginning to congregate around the shop, Billy decided it was time to start work.

Hidalgo was fully illuminated by now. Food merchants had twisted open their propane tanks and oiled their grills. Roving peddlers, hawking bracelets and stylized sets of onyx figurines of toucans, turtles and palmable parrots had begun to scan the bands of tourists, hopeful of making their first sale of the evening. Diminutive Huichol women, dressed in garish mismatched blouses and skirts, accompanied by ever-present babies or toddlers in tow, wound their way through the throng exchanging small boxes of Chicklets for loose change. Children kicked balls. Lean dogs roamed in search of hand-outs.

As Billy positioned himself behind the counter, his first customer appeared within minutes.

"Young man, do you speak English?"

"Yes, ma'am," replied Billy. "May I help you?"

"Well, I'm not sure. I'm interested in this pen with the little iguanas, but I might buy more if you have them."

The speaker appeared to be about seventy years of age. She was short and rail-thin. Her blue-tinged hair was piled high and shellacked hard enough to repel wayward bats or falling coconuts. Gold rings adorned each claw-like finger. An outfit consisting of a loose floral print green top with coordinating blue knee-length shorts did nothing to conceal pale mottled arms and wrinkled spindle shaped legs.

A slightly taller, identically dressed man, capped in a black toupee, hung back a few steps, beaming with anticipation at his mate's forthcoming performance at bartering. He had witnessed the routine before.

Turning toward Assistant, and eager to make his first sale, Billy searched for the correct Spanish words and inquired falteringly: *"Amigo, más plumas con iguanas?"*

"Si, muchos," confirmed Assistant.

"Yes, ma'am. We have more iguana pens if you're interested." Billy began to anticipate a profitable night's work.

"How much would you charge me for five?"

45

snipped the tourist in a dour tone.

From his smirk, Billy could see that the lady's husband was beginning to enjoy the show.

"I'll check again, ma'am. One moment please." The old woman's question had disarmed Billy. Hermano had not discussed the fine art of dickering with him before his departure.

Billy turned toward Assistant once again. *"Cuánto es cinco plumas?"*

"Cinco? Cien Pesos." Assistant regarded Billy as if he had definitely made a bad career choice. Hermano's prices were firm.

Billy relayed the message: "Five pens will cost one-hundred pesos."

"But that's not saving anything! Each pen was marked at twenty pesos!"

"I know, ma'am. I guess our prices are fixed." Billy wished she would simply disappear.

Other people were beginning to slow down to gawk.

Her husband's grin had transformed itself into an open smile.

Assistant shook his head while glancing downward.

"You guess your prices are fixed? That's ridiculous! What kind of a place is this? Everybody in Mexico barters! Do you take me for a fool young man?"

Her barrage was relentless.

"Yes, ma'am. I mean no, ma'am!" Billy now wished *he* could disappear, but not with her.

46

The attack continued.

"You are an insolent young man! Where is the owner? I demand to speak with him immediately! Who is that boy? Let me talk to him!"

"The owner's not here right now, ma'am. He may not be back for hours. The boy and I just work here. He doesn't speak much English."

By now, a small crowd had gathered.

The assailant's spouse resembled a sneering vulture ready to pick ravenously at what was left of Billy's flesh.

Assistant continued to stare at his worn sandals.

Billy prayed for the end of the world.

"Now, let me ask you again!" continued Billy's waking nightmare. "How much will five iguana pens cost me? I'm not leaving until I get an acceptable price from you!" "Mrs. Blue-Hair" realized she had gained the upper hand.

The situation was hopeless. Billy had been beaten by a ninety pound blue shark.

He gestured for his opponent to approach closer. What he had to tell this raging raptor was not for others to overhear. "Listen, lady, I think we can do business here," whispered Billy. "If you give me ninety pesos for five pens, I'll throw in the extra ten pesos from my own pocket. You'll get a bargain, and nobody'll know that I lowered the price. Do we have a deal?"

For the first time that evening, Billy saw his

adversary smile. *Strange,* he thought, *how such tiny dentures could do such a good job of chewing me to pieces.*

The remainder of the shift improved steadily. It had to. By the time Hermano arrived in his pickup around midnight, Billy had sold six coffee cups, four silver plated bracelets, two ash trays and a pair of green sunglasses as well as the pens.

Stepping up from the curb from Avenido México, Hermano seemed pleased that his beloved business remained intact. "Hola, amigos! How did the sales progress for the night?"

"I think we did well, boss," replied Billy, shooting a conspiratorial glance at Assistant. "I kept a list of everything I sold and I know you'll be pleased."

Although not contributing to any of the conversation, Assistant sensed that a smile and a nod were in order. After all, if he and the gringo were to become partners, certain business indiscretions might best be forgotten.

"*Bueno*, Billy!" exclaimed Hermano. "Now the night has the perfection!"

Billy was relieved that the discourse seemed to be taking another turn.

"How was your date with Angelica?" he inquired.

"Oh, Billy," sighed Hermano, "I think I have the love for her."

Billy's eyebrows raised. "What happened, amigo?"

"Well," began the man of business, "first we

48

had the dinner. Angelica had the salad, the steak and the shrimp. I had the soup, the tacos and the chicken. Angelica ate my chicken. She is so beautiful when she eats, Billy! When she chews the food, she opens her mouth and smiles at me with much pleasure. We drank beer and talked. When I told her a funny story, she laughed so hard that the beer flew from her mouth and nose! It made my shirt wet. It was very romantic. I think the stains will come out.

"After the dinner, we went for the long walk along the Malecón. Angelica ate some crêpes with caramelo. When I held her hand, she squeezed mine in return. She was very sticky from the caramelo. She was very sweet.

"Then I took her home. It was a short walk, but all the way my heart was pounding — boom, boom, boom! When we arrived at her door, my mouth had the dryness. I couldn't speak. All I could do was stare at my sweet angel!

"What happened next is most beautiful! We looked at each other in the moonlight and slowly our lips came together. We couldn't seem to pull them apart."

No wonder, thought Billy, *her mouth was probably covered in caramel.*

Hermano continued: "After the kiss, we promised to meet again the night of tomorrow. As I walked to my home to get the truck, it all felt like the dream. I do not remember how I found my own house! Do you think it could be the love, Billy?"

"I'm sure it is, my friend!" answered Billy.

"You didn't eat enough to get heartburn."

Hermano seemed pleased with the profundity of Billy's reply.

Assistant smiled and shrugged.

Together, the three set about loading merchandise onto the back of Hermano's battered truck.

When the task was completed, and the proprietor had carefully placed the cashbox to his right, on the worn passenger side of the seat, he turned to Billy before departing.

"You did well tonight, my friend. The business was good. You and the boy made much profit! I am happy that you are working here. I am happy for the night. *Hasta luego, amigo!*"

"See you soon, friend," replied Billy, "and, thanks."

Hermano smiled at Assistant, said something in rapid Spanish, and drove off into the night.

It was now left to Billy and Assistant to wheel the empty cart back to its assigned parking allocation. The manoeuvring took less than five minutes.

When Assistant was satisfied that all was secure, he turned to Billy with an extended hand. As the two shook, the young apprentice spoke slowly and deliberately: "Good night, Billy."

"Good night, partner."

A trust had been cemented.

During the short walk back to Hallowe'en Street, Billy reflected upon the night's endeavours. Except for the sparring match with Mrs. Blue-Hair at the onset, his first shift had gone well. Billy had enjoyed the work. He had made a friend. He was also pleased that Hermano's burgeoning romance was progressing smoothly.

As he unlocked and swung open the door to his apartment, Billy felt glad to be home. Flicking on the lights and heading to the fridge for a can of Modelo, he realized how good life could be.

Settling in with Responsibilities

At sunset the next evening, Billy arrived at the park ready for work.

His employer and Assistant had already set up the merchandise and were just finishing stringing up the lights.

"Hola, Billy! How are you tonight? Ready to make the work?"

"Hello, boss," Billy answered. "I'm just fine and ready to get going! How are you doing, my friend?"

"I'm good, but sadly, Angelica must work at the *farmacia* tonight. I will stay here with you and also work but, later on, I will visit her and bring my angel the flowers!"

"Sounds good, Hermano! The flowers are a nice touch. I'm told that ladies like roses." Billy winked at Hermano.

Hermano smiled and winked back.

Glancing over at Assistant, who had manned his post behind the stand, Billy touched his cheek under his right eye and nodded in an attempt at emulating Hermano's familiar business gesture. It was delivered with good-natured sport among three friends.

When Assistant responded, his own gesticulation bore an eerie similarity to his employer's own patented move. His face remained earnest.

Hermano smiled proudly.

This is really weird, Billy reflected.

The next few hours passed quickly. Souvenirs and trinkets were sold in abundance to tourists and locals alike. At one point, Hermano even managed to unload a near-perpetual motion toy to a pair of gullible sweethearts with no comprehension of the intricacies of magnetism.

At around ten, Hermano announced that it was now time to pay his respects to Angelica. His heart was ready.

"Would you do me a favour, amigo?" asked Billy, before his friend departed. "Would you ask Angelica if Raquel and Patti are still employed at the drugstore? I think I might like to ask one of them to dinner or something."

"Sure, I will ask. When I return, I will tell you the information."

"Thanks, boss. You go on now. Have a good time. Don't forget the flowers. Assistant and I can look after things."

Satisfied that his new employee could indeed fulfill his duties in a competent manner, Hermano bowed slightly and departed. Love awaited.

"Well, partner, I guess it's you and me now," asserted Billy to Assistant. "Let's make the big boss proud!"

Together, they did.

When Hermano returned about an hour and half later, he appeared in an exceptionally jubilant mood.

"My friends, let us pack the goods a little early tonight! I would very much enjoy to relate about my visit with my Angelica to you! We can drink beer and I can tell you about what my

53

heart is feeling for the future."

"Sounds good to me," agreed Billy. "Let's get started."

Business had been brisk and when the last of the goods was loaded onto Herman's truck, Billy was thankful that work for the night was finished. Potential customers were beginning to drift back to their hotels or homes, and several stores along the main road were in the process of securing their doors.

Once the cart had been vanquished for the evening, Billy suggested they cross the cobblestones to La Scala restaurant, order some cold beer and listen to Hermano's tale. His plan met with no opposition.

When the three were comfortably seated at a corner table overlooking the street, and refreshments had been ordered, Billy was the first to speak. "So, tell us, my friend, what happened with you and Angelica tonight?"

"Well," replied Hermano, " I listened to your advice. When I walked into the *farmacia* with the flowers I had purchased, Angelica was standing behind the counter sticking the price tags onto the jars of baby food. She didn't see me at first, but when she did look up and saw me standing there, her smile made me forget where I was. Her white uniform made her look even more like an angel than ever!

"I looked around the store to see that no other peoples had come in, then leaned over the counter and kissed her. Her lips were so sweet! I wondered if she had been eating the candy. It was then I noticed many empty wrappers on the shelf behind her.

"After the kiss, I gave her the flowers. She smiled again and stuck one behind her ear. I'm sure you were right about the roses, Billy, but we forgot about the thorns! Anyway, her ear didn't bleed that much.

" When she stopped crying, I asked her if she would like to go to the special dinner Saturday night. This made her feel much more better. I think, that at the dinner, I will tell her of my love!"

"Just go slowly," advised Billy. "There's no sense rushing into things."

"I know you are probably right, amigo, but there was something about Angelica handling the jars of baby food with such tenderness that it put great thoughts of the fathering into my mind."

Throughout his mentor's entire dissertation, Assistant had sat in silence, sipping his Coke and glancing about the restaurant with seeming indifference. Immediately following Hermano's last assertion however, a coughing spell gripped the young man so severely that his face reddened and breaths were stolen in quick gasps.

The sudden change in demeanor was short - lived however, and within several seconds, Assistant seemed to regain his bearings.

"Are you okay, buddy?" Billy asked with genuine concern.

"The composure is back. Thanks, Billy."

Billy's suspicions that Assistant's comprehension of spoken English was far greater than he revealed were now confirmed.

Hermano, appearing greatly relieved, rose from his chair, bent and hugged his young protégé, and whispered something in his ear in soothing Spanish phrases.

Whatever was said seemed to appease Assistant completely and he now seemed ready to resume the evening with typical aloofness.

Billy however, thought a change in subject matter might be warranted.

"Hermano, did you get a chance to ask about Patti and Raquel?"

"Si, I did. Just before I left the *farmacia*, I asked. It seems like the jobs in Mexico City pay a lot more."

"Oh well, thanks anyway. I was just curious," responded Billy, visibly disappointed.

Assistant remained silent, but met Billy's eyes, smiled and shrugged as if to say, "Don't worry, lots of fish in the sea."

You're right, thought Billy. This time, it was his turn to smile and shrug.

The remainder of the evening passed uneventfully. Talk of business ensued. Several more *cervezas* were consumed.

Finally, Hermano rose to take his leave. *"Buenas noches, amigos. I must leave now, but I will see you tomorrow at the work."*

With that assertion, the three shook hands and Hidalgo's colorful bursar departed for his securely locked old pickup parked in full view across the street.

"Well, Assistant, I guess I'll get going too. It was a good night."

"Me too, Billy. We worked very hard tonight."

Once on the street, the two young men shook hands before seeking separate ways.

"Just a minute, amigo. Before you go, there's something that's been driving me crazy. May I ask you a question?" Billy inquired respectfully.

"Si."

"We work together now, and I don't even know your name. *Cómo se llamo?*" asked Billy in his best Spanish.

"My name is Hermano," answered the fledgling salesman with profuse self-respect.

The two shook again and departed company for the evening.

Throughout the short walk back to his apartment, Billy couldn't help pondering the intricacies of human relationships. The two Hermanos had triggered his thoughts. Arriving at his door, the transplanted American impassively concluded that life was indeed a puzzle. Sometimes, things made no sense. That was just the way it was. So be it.

Routines and Changes

Billy was happy. He continued to enjoy exploring the city by day and pushing his wares in the park by night.

To him, his job was considered a joyful experience. Each evening, he looked forward to meeting new people and working with his friends. Billy also realized that after years of drifting aimlessly through each day, structure was now something he welcomed.

His Spanish was improving on a daily basis. During each shift, he and the young Hermano managed to find time, during lulls in business, to pose questions to each other and exchange information concerning vocabulary and grammatical structures of their respective languages. When they spoke, it was often in a combination of Spanish and English. Both were fast learners.

The musician was changing in other facets as well.

Physical transformation had also occurred. Because of his arduous ramblings, sinuey muscle now covered much of Billy's lanky body. The sun had stained him to a degree where he was now darker than many native Mexicans. Billy's sun - bleached hair and pale eyes contrasted strikingly with his bronze complexion.

His old running shoes had not yet fallen apart and cut-off jeans and tank tops remained the preferred wardrobe . The only adornments Billy now possessed were a silver ring depicting the Aztec calendar and a string necklace consisting of three turquoise beads. Both had been purchased at Hermano's stand. A wristwatch wasn't necessary. Time wasn't as important as it was in the States.

Gone were the days of hazy recollections brought about through excesses in whatever substance seemed convenient. Mexican beer was the only vice Billy now favored, and even that was consumed, *for the most part*, in limited quantities.

Billy had no complaints. He lived in paradise, had friends and took great pleasure in his job. *Still...*

A Gem

After a week of working at the shop, Billy found himself busily engaged in trying to repair a faulty extension cord which was causing their string of lights to burn out at a maddening pace.

Assistant was attempting to sell a pair of red plastic sandals to a tourist from Ohio.

Hermano was courting an angel.

Suddenly, Billy's task was interrupted.

"Pardon me. Could you help us please?"

Putting the pliers aside, he turned to face the voice.

"Yes, miss?" Billy inquired somewhat disarmed by the appearance of the speaker.

She was tall with wavy , shoulder-length blonde hair, a small delicate nose, pouting lips and large, expressive hazel eyes. Her short green skirt and white sleeveless top did nothing to conceal her tanned legs and other ample charms.

She spoke again. "We were wondering how much these little change purses were. It's impossible to keep track of all the coins here."

Billy now noticed there were three other girls accompanying the pretty young blonde — all in their early twenties, all very attractive.

"They're ten pesos apiece, miss, but if you were to buy four, I could let you have them all for thirty pesos." Billy had no idea why he voluntarily discounted the price, but, for the second time in a week, he would have to make up the difference from his own pocket.

As pesos and purses were exchanged, Billy found himself suddenly wanting to know more about the identity of his newest customer.

"Are you from one of the cruise ships, miss?"

"No, we're from Canada, on a break from college. We flew in a couple of days ago from Toronto and are here for nearly two more weeks. We love it! Everyone is so nice and the town is beautiful! Do you live here?"

"Yes, but I'm originally from Chicago," Billy replied. "I can't think of anywhere else in the world I'd rather be though. For me, this is home. Where are you people staying?"

"We're just down the street at the Rosita," she answered, a slight smile appearing on her lips. "It's clean, the people are friendly, and it sure has lots of character."

Billy, encouraged by her smile and open manner of speaking, decided to press on. "You're right. I often sit on the breakwall beside the hotel and watch the fishermen. They work hard and I work hard at watching them."

The young woman laughed and Billy felt elated.

By this time, several potential customers had begun to congregate in front of the shop and Assistant was beckoning Billy with pleading glances to help out with the overflow.

"It's been really nice talking with you, but I guess I'd better look after some other customers before my partner has a breakdown," Billy uttered almost apologetically. "Hope you have a good night."

"Thanks, you too. We'll probably see you before we have to leave. See you later."

"I sure hope so!" Billy blurted out, without thinking.

Again, she smiled, and with her friends, set off in a southerly direction, perhaps with the Malecón as their intended destination. Having proceeded about ten paces, the tall blonde turned, faced Billy, who had been watching her depart, and called back: "By the way, my name's Ruby!"

"Mine's Billy!"

She pivoted again, and with the other girls, crossed Langarica.

Billy followed her every step with unbridled attention.

For the guitar player from Chicago, the remainder of the evening passed in a blur. Money and trinkets traded hands and profits were made.

Assistant found himself shaking his head in amused disbelief as he caught his partner searching for Ruby in the crowd.

Hermano made several brief appearances throughout the night, but appeared too distracted to remain at business for very long. Judging from his constant smile, Angelica was simply too alluring.

At around mid-night, the ever-animated proprietor returned to Hidalgo for the final time of the evening. His face was smeared with bright red lipstick. It was candy apple red.

Goods were packed. The cart was stored.

Before leaving with the cash box, Hermano turned to Billy and Assistant: "It's been a good week, amigos! I have the wages ready for you." After completing his customary business gesture, Hermano broke into a wide smile while examining the finger which had touched his cheek. He sighed deeply and handed each of his employees a sealed envelope.

Billy thanked him and tucked his pay into the pocket of his worn cut-offs. To examine the contents of the envelope at this time would appear highly inopportune.

The three adjourned.

Later, sitting at his own kitchen table and sipping a night cap of Modelo, Billy opened his pay envelope. He was surprised at the number of pesos it contained. After making some quick mathematical conversions however, he calculated the sum to equal approximately seventeen dollars in American currency. *Damn good thing I'm on a budget,* he thought.

Draining the last drops of beer from the can, Billy Emmerson decided to get some sleep. There were things he had to do in the morning.

Something to Think About

I wanna close my eyes at night,
And think of you.
I wanna open 'em in the morning,
Still be thinkin' of you.
Oh, woman!
That's all I wanna do!

- Big Nose Jefferson, 1956

Billy awoke early the next morning, showered, shaved, and dressed in a clean pair of cut-offs and a new white T-shirt. After his second cup of black coffee, he locked the door of his apartment and descended the cobblestones of Hallowe'en Street.

Before crossing Ordaz, he decided to pay a brief visit to Paco's convenience store. It was still early.

As he entered, Billy was pleased to see his friend standing behind the counter, ready for business.

"Morning, Paco! How're you doing?"

"Good, Billy. How 'bout you, my friend?"

"I'm good. Working with Hermano at the park now. I really like it. Meet lots of people there." Billy smiled.

"That's okay! Good for you, amigo!" exclaimed Paco. "Keeps you out of trouble. Are you still in love with the two señoritas from the drugstore? *That* could be trouble, my friend!"

"No. I heard they moved to Mexico City to get better jobs," Billy answered with exaggerated detachment.

"Oh, well, maybe it's better. Want a beer, Billy?"

"No thanks. It's a little early. I just stepped in to see how you were doing. I really have to get going. See you later!"

The young Mr. Emmerson was thankful that Paco didn't question his hasty departure.

It was a short walk from Paco's to the break wall just outside the fenced-in pool area of the Hotel Rosita.

From this location, while positioned on his favorite boulder, Billy could follow the activities of the fishermen, and by simply standing and turning, could easily ascertain the presence of those at poolside. It seemed like the perfect plan. All Billy had to do was to periodically check to see if Ruby and her friends were swimming or lounging around the deck. He could then, very casually, stroll up to the fence and initiate a conversation. He had told Ruby that he enjoyed watching the fishermen. It would all seem quite coincidental. It was foolproof!

The first hour passed with no sign of Ruby or her friends.

Billy watched the fishing boats come and go, nets being repaired, and hungry, fat pelicans eagerly devouring scraps of tossed aside visceral.

One particularly hungry bird reminded Billy a lot of Frank Levinski, without the cigar.

At around eleven, the man with the plan decided to stretch his legs and retrieve something cold to drink from Paco's corner store. The sun was rising rapidly and Billy could feel beads of perspiration begin to trickle down his forehead. Before leaving, he turned to once again peruse the pool in hopes of glimpsing the blonde student who had occupied his thoughts incessantly since the night before. His searching eyes were met by someone instantly recognizable, but not Ruby!

"Holy Christ! Please say it's not her!" Billy exclaimed in a whisper.

From the fenced-in pool area, about twenty feet from where Billy now stood motionless, came the shriek of an enraged jackal: "And just what do you think you're staring at, young man! Why aren't you working? Don't you have anything better to do than to spy upon people?" It was Mrs. Blue-Hair.

Sensing that he was in for an unscheduled display of great magnitude, Mrs. Blue-Hair's skinny-legged husband slithered closer to his mate to be nearer the action when it erupted. He was wise enough however to maintain a slight distance from his spouse. He didn't want to stray too near her snapping jaws. Billy hoped his toupee would cause him severe sunstroke.

There's no way I'm gonna get in another fight with that woman, thought Billy. *I've got better things to think about!*

"Answer me, young man!" snipped Mrs. Blue-Hair.

"Have a nice day, ma'am!" replied Billy with exaggerated courtesy.

Mrs. Blue-Hair recoiled unabashedly at what she construed as the young vendor's gracious rejoinder.

While she remained silent and open-mouthed, Billy bowed ever so slightly to her, turned, and left toward Paco's.

Returning to man his post twenty minutes later, the chivalrous Mr. Emmerson was pleased that Mrs. Blue-Hair and her mate were nowhere to be seen. The cold beer had refreshed him. Billy was once again ready to resume his quest.

His strategy soon proved successful. The results were worth the waiting.

"Good morning, Billy!"

Rising from his rocky perch and turning toward the hotel, Billy was rewarded with the sight of Ruby standing just inside the fence and waving to him.

"Hi!" shouted Billy. *Bikinis should be made mandatory for people who look like her,* he thought, as he approached the enclosure.

"I thought it was you when I looked out at the fishing boats, but I wasn't sure," said Ruby as Billy drew nearer.

"Yep, it's a big part of my busy lifestyle," Billy replied. He now stood directly in front of Ruby.

"Would you like to come in and join my friends and me for something to eat?"

"No...Thanks anyway," answered Billy, not

wanting to appear too pushy. "I'd better get going. This afternoon, I promised myself to go iguana watching at the Rio Cuale."

"Sounds like fun!"

"Yeah, it can get pretty fast-paced alright!" Ruby laughed.

Billy felt encouraged.

"Do you think you'll be around the park tonight?" He decided he had nothing to lose by posing the question directly.

"It's hard to say. I don't know what the others want to do. I think it's really pretty there and I sure wouldn't mind going back."

"Well, maybe I'll see you later then," Billy answered with undisguised hope in his voice.

"Sounds really nice."

"Okay, Ruby."

With that, Billy smiled, waved shyly to the young woman, and set out toward Ordaz.

Ruby had returned his parting gestures before he left.

He was still smiling when he arrived at the Rio Cuale.

Iguana spotting had never been more enjoyable.

Business Not as Usual

When Billy reported for work that evening, he was gratified to note that his portly employer had positioned himself in front of the shop and was busily engaged in finalizing the sale of six, matching shot glasses, emblazoned with the words: "For Tequila Only!" Perhaps Hermano would join his co-workers for more than a few brief periods throughout the night. If so, Billy speculated, he might be given the opportunity to slip off and talk to Ruby if she appeared.

Once greetings had been exchanged, the novice salesman situated himself beside Assistant, behind the counter, and began his nightly endeavors.

Transactions progressed well, but Billy found himself anxiously scanning the crowd, whenever there was a break, in search of Ruby. His surreptitious deeds did not go unnoticed by his partner who reacted by smiling to himself and shaking his head as if to silently assert that the running of the business seemed to fall entirely upon his young shoulders tonight.

Halfway through the shift, Billy spotted Ruby wandering through the crowd and approaching the cart from the general vicinity of Langarica.

When eye contact had been established, Billy hurriedly excused himself from his friends and met her about midway between the store and the street.

"Hi, Ruby."

"Hi, Billy."

"Where are your friends tonight?" asked Billy, inwardly thankful the pretty Canadian seemed to be alone.

"We all went to La Scala for dinner, but I decided to skip dessert and cross over to see what was happening."

Billy felt like a million pesos. *Why not?* he thought. *Here goes nothing!*

"Look, Ruby," he began, "I know we just met and everything and I know you don't even know me, but I was wondering if...maybe we could get together for lunch or...get married or something if you like."

Ruby grinned at Billy's last proposal, but was not to be intimidated by the young man's bravado. "Tomorrow is good for me, Billy, if it's okay with you. Why don't you come by the Rosita around ten and we could go for a long walk on the beach and hunt for shells? Maybe we could talk about marriage the next day."

In response, a lopsided grin and blush appeared on Billy's tanned face.

"That sounds really good," he stammered. "What if I meet you just outside the fence by the beach?"

"I'll be there at ten," replied Ruby, looking directly into Billy's blue eyes.

"Well, I guess I'd better get back to work then. We're pretty busy tonight." Billy paused briefly , then added: "I'm glad you came over to the park tonight, Ruby, and I'm glad I'm seeing you tomorrow."

"Me too, Billy. See you tomorrow."

Ruby turned away slowly and began the short walk back to her friends.

Billy followed her every step.

Returning to the workplace, he was met by a beaming Hermano who seemed to take great pleasure in Billy's romantic interlude.

Assistant merely shook his head.

Tall Talk on a Short Walk

At a few minutes before ten the next morning, an apprehensive American found himself standing near the breakwall of the Hotel Rosita, just outside the fenced-in pool area on the beach side. It was a brief, direct amble down from Hallowe'en Street, but he didn't remember making contact with the cobblestones that morning. His mind was swimming with loftier matters. *I wonder what she'll be wearing,* he thought.

As Billy stared out at the Pacific and reflected upon such thoughts, his daydreaming was suddenly, but pleasantly disrupted.

"Good morning, Billy."

It was the voice of the object of his contemplation.

Ruby had emerged from the front lobby of the hotel a moment before, and had turned right a few paces onto Ordaz. A few more steps to the west brought Billy and Bandaras Bay directly into her view.

Billy turned to face Ruby and greeted her with a smile and his own, "Good morning!"

The question of her attire was now answered. Standing before Billy, the tall, lithe tourist was dressed simply and appropriately for the morning's outing, at least in Billy's humble opinion. Ruby's sandals appeared broken-in and comfortable. Her short, tight cut-offs clung like a second skin to a slim waist and a perfectly curved posterior which reminded Billy of the shape of an inverted heart.

A black, sleeveless blouse, buttoned up the front, confirmed what he had hoped for and imagined. Her firm breasts needed no artificial support. *Yes,* thought Billy, *she couldn't have chosen her wardrobe any better!*

"You look really pretty this morning, Ruby. I'm glad you're wearing sandals too. Sometimes the tide washes in bits of broken glass. You sure wouldn't want to step on them with bare feet!" Billy thought his compliment seemed quite unobtrusive. He didn't believe it prudent to expound upon the wonders of her other articles of clothing.

"Thanks, kind sir. It sure looks like a good morning for a walk. Do you think we'll find anything interesting?"

"Oh, I'm sure we will. I always do."

The two young people proceeded in a southerly direction, following the sand bordering the Pacific side of the Malecón.

It didn't take them long to begin to feel comfortable in each other's presence.

At times, an unexpected wave would splash playfully over their shoes as they bent to examine some small treasure. Both would laugh as they scrambled to higher ground. Both knew the scene would be repeated throughout the morning. Neither one minded in the least.

Between small talk and child-like bursts of enthusiasm when shells or polished pieces of glass were discovered, each, through the genuine urgings of the other, would reveal pieces of his or her personal history.

Ruby spoke of a typical middle-class upbringing in a small town a couple of hours from Toronto, her high school life, and the year and a half spent working full-time at various mediocre jobs in order to save money for college. In another year, she hoped to graduate and find employment in a publishing house. She loved books and believed the job would ideally suit her personality.

She also opened up to Billy on an unexpected emotional level. Ruby felt at ease confiding in him. Maybe, because he was a virtual stranger. Maybe, it was because he was someone who really seemed to listen.

She told Billy of a recent relationship which had gone bad too soon. Mismatched personalities, lack of trust, and broken promises were all factors which contributed to the breakup.

As Ruby, with mounting confidence, peeled away layers of her own character, Billy felt his respect for her honesty increasing as each stone was uncovered.

Spurred on by her example, the young man found himself discussing details of his own life which had been buried for months. Maybe, it was catharsis. Maybe, it was the girl.

He told her of his struggling days as a musician in Chicago, and of how the meteoric rise of "Hard Driven Rain" had propelled The

Squires from a club band to pseudo rock stars almost overnight.

Billy spoke of David Hanson and Frank Levinski.

He told Ruby about the good times and the bad.

He confessed his cynicism and eventual disillusionment with his life at the time, and his decision to escape to "someplace warm."

Mentally, Billy began to draw parallels between Ruby's failed relationship and the time he had spent with Lizzy Blair, but decided that any similarities between the two concepts seemed greatly out of proportion. He let the idea drop.

Finally, with the passion of youth, Billy expounded upon his love for Mexico, its people, and the simple fulfilled life Vallarta had offered him. He spoke the words of a man who was beginning to understand himself.

When the two returned to the Rosita shortly after one, they were holding hands. Soft words and glances were exchanged. As they lingered near the front entrance of the hotel, they hugged briefly before resuming their separate rituals for the day.

In the Blinking of a Blue Eye

For Billy Emmerson, the next several days passed fleetingly.

During the days, he and Ruby would spend as much time together as possible. They both enjoyed the beauty of Vallarta and its sultry, surrounding environs and numerous hours were whiled away rambling the city streets, exploring the mountains, beach combing, or simply sitting on a boulder at the breakwall and gazing at the Pacific.

This may not be love, Billy thought, *but it's damned close to it.*

At work each night, the smiling salesman good-naturedly accepted every barbed innuendo Hermano shot at him concerning his little blonde *chica.* When the barrage became too distracting however, Billy could always silence his employer by questioning him with feigned severity, about Angelica's fidelity. The gibes were always given and taken in the spirit of kinship.

Throughout these exchanges, Assistant would simply shake his head and conduct business as usual.

What a Difference a Day Makes

On the Monday afternoon, marking the closing of Ruby's vacation in the sun, she reluctantly informed her constant companion that her plane would be departing at two the next afternoon.

At the time, she and Billy were engaged in constructing a sand castle on the beach opposite the Malecón. Suddenly, Billy didn't feel like continuing the endeavor.

"I thought it was tomorrow, but I was hoping I was wrong," murmured Billy with remorse surfacing in his voice.

"I don't want to leave, Billy. I think these last two weeks have been wonderful. Let's not even talk about it now. We still have twenty-four hours left so let's make the most of them."

When Ruby had finished speaking, Billy took her hands in his and looked at her without attempting a reply.

Ruby's eyes began to cloud over.

Finally, Billy responded. "You're right. It's been great for me too. I just don't want it to end." He paused momentarily, then added: "I'm going to leave word at the park that I won't be working tonight. My boss is a good guy. There won't be any problem. We can go somewhere for dinner where it's quiet. I'll even buy you a cheeseburger! We can talk and have a few beers. Does that sound okay, Ruby?"

"It sounds more than okay, Billy." Ruby attempted a smile, but her voice betrayed her reluctance to accept the termination of what had become a warm, supportive relationship.

Plans were consolidated. Billy walked Ruby to the front entrance of her hotel.

When he returned a couple of hours later, Billy saw Ruby waiting in the lobby before she noticed him.

He was amazed at the transformation she had undergone in such a short period of time. Gone were the sandals and cut-offs. Ruby was now attired in a full-length sky-blue dress, accentuated with delicate embroidered floral designs surrounding puffed short sleeves, hem, and a modest neck line. Her blonde hair was pulled back, wrapped, and secured with an ivory comb. She was polished.

She noticed Billy.

They left.

Dinner was good.

The conversation was better.

Too quickly however, the evening was drawing to a close.

Ruby in the Sky

I know that you don't love me,
But lie to me tonight.
Tell me that you need me,
And in the morning light,
You can leave my bedside,
While I pretend to sleep,
But don't make empty promises,
You don't intend to keep.

-Melissa Dawn May, 1976

The moment that Billy had dreaded throughout the evening, had now become reality.

Standing before the open lobby of the Hotel Rosita, he reached for Ruby's hands and peered into her eyes for the second time that day. Again, words escaped him.

It was Ruby who broke the spell. "I talked to my roommate, Billy. She's staying with my other two friends. You're not leaving."

Billy didn't leave.

Ruby was a diamond.

Keepin' On

Days and weeks passed for Billy Emmerson with no signs of abatement for the wonder and the attachment he felt toward his adopted land and its people. There were always new corners of the city to discover, new jungle trails to explore, and new and interesting people to meet.

He still enjoyed his job in Parque Hidalgo, but often wished his pay envelope were a bit plumper. Billy could not exist solely on what he earned and often had to dip into the savings Frank Levinski had wisely set aside for each of the Squires when times were good.

Thanks, in great part, to Assistant's patient coaching, the former resident of Chicago could now understand most simple conversations in Spanish, provided they weren't delivered in rapid syllables.

Over the months, his relationship with Hermano had reached a point of comfortable homeostasis. The pair would often share meals or drink beer together after work for an hour or two, but there were certain boundaries neither crossed in respect for the other's domain.

Billy still didn't know to what destination his friend vanished every night once the truck had been loaded and the cash box stowed. He had no conception of what Hermano's life was like during the hours of sunlight.

In a reciprocal manner, Hermano had never questioned Billy about his life before Vallarta.

Intrinsically, he felt that if his young employee had wanted to discuss his past, he would have done so.

Hermano knew that Billy lived somewhere up on Calle 31 de Octubre, but had never visited him or had never even remotely thought of arriving uninvited.

When Ruby had flown home several months ago, the bantering in the park, however innocent, had ceased immediately. To Hermano, invading a friend's privacy was completely unthinkable.

Mexican gentility.

An Idea Begins to Germinate

On a hot, humid morning in July, Billy was enjoying his coffee while doing nothing more than leisurely examining the bent old tamarind tree sprawling outside his kitchen window. Suddenly the realization came to him that it would soon be a year since his arrival in Mexico. Perhaps the familiar tree had pried his memory. Billy knew that the month was July, but had to consult the calendar attached to his fridge door with a dolphin-shaped magnet, in order to ascertain the exact date. Time moved differently in Mexico. *God*, thought Billy, *I can't believe I've been here a year come tomorrow!*

In some respects, the days had passed quickly for Billy. There was always something in which to take delight. Because of his almost immediate sense of belonging however, he felt that he had been a part of Vallarta his entire life.

Finishing his coffee, and placing his cup in the sink to soak, Billy decided it might be a good day to replenish his dwindling supply of groceries. Since the morning had turned overcast and the moisture laden air had now given way to an invasive mist, strenuous outdoor activities seemed far from appealing.

Several small markets or *mercados* were scattered throughout the immediate neighborhood and usually supplied enough variety to satisfy Billy's culinary requirements. Today however, because of the oppressive weather conditions, he decided to take a bus to the large, air-conditioned supermarket several kilometres toward the airport and take his time purchasing supplies.

After several stops to accept and discharge passengers, the blue and white dinosaur pulled up at curbside and Billy exited near the glassed-in front of the modern food facility.

Entering and passing under an arbor shaped security scanner, he selected the nearest buggy available and began his perambulation through the labyrinth of aisles.

The young man's needs were few, but there was no reason to hurriedly purchase his staples. He enjoyed the cool comfort of the store and much preferred this environment to the sticky conditions on the outside.

Finally Billy decided he could no longer dawdle and wheeled his purchases to the express line. Cheese, peanut butter, wieners, buns and ground beef were squeezed into one bag. Other items such as eggs, fresh vegetables and seafood could be obtained closer to home on another day. Even after a year, Billy could not seem to cultivate a taste for the more traditional and spicy foods of his adopted homeland. A juicy cheeseburger was opted over a taco on any occasion.

Passing through another security scanner near the exit, the selective shopper stepped outside and immediately wished he had never left the supermarket. The air was even heavier than it had been forty-five minutes ago.

As Billy crossed the street to catch a bus, he looked forward to returning to his home, switching on the ceiling fan, taking a long, cool shower, and cracking open a can of Modelo.

Within minutes, a bus marked, "Centro" pulled up to the curb. Billy stepped in, paid his fare and was lucky enough to find a vacant seat about halfway down the aisle. Opening the window, he hoped there wouldn't be too many stops on the way back home.

At the second stop, about five minutes into transit, Billy noticed a young Mexican, carrying a guitar, step aboard and exchange a few words with the driver. The driver nodded and the young man made his way to the back.

These travelling musicians were a common sight and Billy had often heard them perform while commuting by bus. They would play two or three songs, gratefully accept loose change from the riders, depart a few stops down the line, and resume the same routine on another bus. They were usually quite entertaining. Billy would always donate a few pesos as a token of his appreciation. By the end of the day, these hard-working *músicos* could earn a very comfortable living.

The newly-boarded young man assumed a balanced stance, strummed a few soft chords, and broke into a ballad that immediately caught Billy's attention. After a few bars, it was readily apparent to the lapsed guitar player from a land away, that he was witnessing a display of rare talent. Although the young crooner was far more than an adequate singer and musician, there appeared a timbre in his delivery that transcended anything Billy had ever heard.

By the end of the first song, many passengers had shifted their positions to better view the performer. As the last note faded, a smattering of applause followed. Billy felt he deserved much more.

By the end of the second song, Billy realized how wrong he had been in deeming this man to be talented. He was remarkable. This time the applause was greater. Billy felt he deserved much, much more.

Billy sat in revelation. He had missed playing his music — not the showmanship and glitter, but playing for the shear intrinsic good feeling the music provided. It took an experience like this to drive home the point.

By the time Billy stepped down from the bus near Hallowe'en and Ordaz, the clouds had cleared. The sun had emerged and a breeze from the Pacific had dispersed the oppressive humidity.

An idea was beginning to germinate in Billy's mind. It was going to be a good day.

An Idea Grows

That night at the park, during a break in commerce, Billy approached his beefy boss with a question: "Hermano, do you know of a store nearby that sells musical instruments? I've never seen one around here." Billy tried to seem very casual.

"Why, my friend? Are you thinking of making the purchase of something?" Hermano's curiosity was broached.

"Well, actually, I'm looking for a guitar," said Billy, "I used to play a bit, you know, and I thought it might be fun to kinda get back into it."

"I've seen the *guitarras* for sale at the Plaza Malecón," replied Hermano, "but not for awhile though." The affable merchant paused briefly and added: "About fifteen years age, my uncle gave me a guitar he won in a poker game up in Tijuana. I learned a little, but lost the interest when I realized my fingers were not of the very good length. It's around somewhere. It has the case and extra strings too. It's yours if you want it, amigo."

"No, no, I couldn't just take it," Billy protested, touched by his employer's generosity. "Maybe I could give you so many pesos a week for it, and that way, I could buy it from you." He did not want to take advantage of Hermano's friendship.

Hermano was well aware of Billy's financial situation, but didn't want his friend to feel embarrassed or uncomfortable in any way. "Okay. How does, let's say, twenty pesos in one week sound to you?" He hoped Billy would accept his paltry schedule of payment.

"Sounds great! I really appreciate it." Billy knew his employer was a much better businessman than this, but under the present circumstances...

The two shook hands to close the deal.

"I'll bring the guitar with me to the park tomorrow night and you can see if you like it," said Hermano.

"Thanks, amigo." Billy knew he owed Hermano more.

The rest of the shift passed typically. Hermano would come and go, dividing his responsibilities between business and his love life with equal intensity. Billy and Assistant would cajole and practice their English and Spanish language skills between sales.

Tonight however, when his partner was occupied in trade, or when he was free for a moment, Billy found himself mentally reviewing the music and lyrics to several of his old songs. On more than one occasion, he caught himself tapping his foot and humming tunes.

Hours later, back at his apartment, the ex-Squire's imagination had taken such a hold on him that sleep seemed impossible. There were ideas defusing in his mind, that with a little effort could be transformed into words and melodies. For the first time in his new life, Billy felt the creative process returning. Extending roots.

Billy Meets Old Lady Martin

Despite a restless night of half-formed dreams and disjointed thoughts, Billy awoke feeling invigorated.

He hoped the hours would pass quickly until at last he could report to work, meet with his boss, and take possession of his new instrument. It had been over a year since Billy had touched a guitar. He anticipated the event like a child waiting for Santa on Christmas Eve.

Finally, dusk fell on Vallarta. Colors of reds, pinks, purples and, blues seemed to cast the city in a subtle radiance of natural warmth and energy. The headlights of buses and taxis appeared like the yellow eyes of predators roaming the mountainous wilderness to the east. Restaurants along Ordaz were in full swing. Odors of garlic, butter, and frying onions assailed the senses of each passerby, enticing him with a promise of even greater hedonistic rewards.

It was time for Billy to depart. The day had seemed like an eternity.

After a few minutes saunter down Hallowe'en to Ordaz, he turned right onto Langarica, crossed the street, and climbed the few steps leading into Hidalgo.

Because the crowd had not yet filled the park, Billy had an unobstructed view of the souvenir stand from his vantage point atop the steps. Assistant appeared to be engrossed in discovering the perpetually faulty bulb which caused all others on the string to flicker sporadically. Hermano stood in front of his *tienda,* arms crossed over his belly and smiling enticingly at a smattering of tourists approaching from Calle Venezuela.

As Billy neared and was spotted by his employer, it was Hermano who spoke first: "Good evening, my friend. How are you on this beautiful night?"

"I'm good! Bright-eyed and ready to work. How are you? Seeing Angelica tonight?"

"Oh yes, Billy! Each day, the love for her grows stronger. My heart pounds like the big drum. My throat is dry like the desert. My stomach feels like I have eaten the tacos and the *frijoles* re-fried for many, many hours!" Hermano was a man of insatiable appetites.

"Sounds like you've got it bad, boss," replied Billy with exaggerated sympathy.

Assistant, taking time out from his electrical dilemma, turned, looked at Billy, shook his head imperceptibly, and resumed his task. He was a young man of few words, but much understanding.

Billy Emmerson was anxious, but not sure how to broach the subject of Hermano's guitar. He was somewhat hesitant about placing too much importance on the matter lest Hermano might feel it was taking precedent over work at the stand. He also felt, that in some way, it might offend his friend if he seemed too quick to remind him of a promise.

Billy's trepidations were soon assuaged.

"Oh, I almost forgot something, my friend! I found the guitar and brought it here for you to see if it is acceptable. It is under the counter in the case." Hermano attempted to appear nonchalant.

"Oh, man that's great! *Muchos gracias!*" Billy made no attempt to appear non-commital.

Stepping around to the back of the cart, Billy glanced under the counter and discovered his new acquisition. Wrapping his hand around the thick plastic handle, he withdrew a dark brown leather case from under the shelf and gently placed it in the area in which he and Assistant stood to sell their trinkets. The case was tattered and scratched, but not gouged or ripped. He now had room to open it.

Hermano and Assistant, by this time, had approached the back of the stand and stood grinning as their friend crouched to unloosen the hinges. Snapping apart the three brass clasps, Billy raised the top carefully and beheld the instrument for the first time. A smile slowly spread across his face as he realized what he had uncovered.

The Martin acoustic was vintage, but in pristine condition. As Billy lifted it from its felt bed, he knew that he and this guitar could make music. He also realized that the strings were stretched and loose. They would need replacing. That was inconsequential. That would come later. When properly tuned, this guitar would sing.

Rising and facing Hermano, Billy met his friend's eyes and quietly spoke his gratitude: "Thank you. She's beautiful."

"You're welcome, Billy. Treat her well."

Benign Blisters

The next few weeks became a frenzied merry-go-round ride for the young American refugee.

During the evenings, he continued to work at the souvenir stand. He enjoyed earning his livelihood with people he liked in a setting he considered ideal.

Throughout the daylight hours, Billy would try to circumvent the mundane in order to immerse himself into what he considered his true avocation. The music had once again captured a vice-like grip on his imagination.

Once three of the strings on the Martin had been replaced by unused ones Billy had discovered in the pick compartment of the case, and the instrument had been tuned, the musician and his guitar became inextricable.

He practiced until his fingers became too tender to form chords. At that point, he would compose new lyrics and hum the melodies to himself.

Soon, the fingertips of his left hand hardened, and words and music began to flow simultaneously.

By the end of the month, Billy had written five new songs and had adapted several of The Squires' old tunes to the acoustic guitar. He was pleased with his accomplishments. He was refining a coarse of action.

The Gringo Lays Down His Cards

During a quiet night in Hidalgo, a few days later, Billy decided to openly confront his employer.

Hermano had learned to dine alone before his courtship ritual with Angelica had resumed for the evening. He was not ready to seek additional employment for the sake of appeasing one of her porcine appetites. Although deeply smitten, he was trying to balance practicality with a growing sense of obligation for fulfilling Angelica's gastronomical needs. The affable entrepreneur usually ate at the park. The food was good, and he could keep sight of business.

Billy approached the businessman as he was busily wiping the remnants of strawberry jam from the corners of his mouth. Angelica had taught him to relish the sweet crêpes made at a nearby stand.

"Hermano, have you got a minute? I've got a business proposition you might be interested in." Billy understood what the word "business" meant to his boss and was pleased when Hermano touched the sacred spot under his right eye and faced him with rapt attention.

"Listen, amigo," began a hopeful Billy. "There are times when business is a little bit slack here. You're often off somewhere with your beautiful lady friend and Assistant and I stand around practicing languages until some tourists show up. Sometimes even then, one person could, at least for a little while, probably handle the work. What if I told you I have an idea to make us all a few extra pesos and it wouldn't cost you anything?"

Hermano seemed intrigued.

Assistant stopped arranging ashtrays in order to tune in to the conversation.

"My ears are open for you! Go ahead, my friend," replied Hermano.

"You know how much I like it here," began Billy, "and you know how much I appreciate my job, but, even more, how I appreciate the guitar you found for me.

"Back in the States, that's what I did for a living. I played guitar and sang songs. I was pretty good, but things went wrong. I came to Mexico to start over again. I was lucky. I found what I was looking for and don't regret my decision for a minute. I can't wait to get up in the morning just to see the sun rising. I have friends who care about me and accept me for what I am."

The young man found himself surprised at how much of himself he was suddenly revealing, but continued to let his thoughts pour out. He hadn't talked so much since confiding in Ruby.

Both of his friends remained silent.

"I'm not sure what I'm really trying to say right now so maybe I'd better just get to the point. What if I brought my guitar to the park and played a few songs when business is slow? If the people like the songs, maybe they'd spare some change and we could split it up like we do selling things here. Assistant would have to cover for me a bit at times, but we would all profit in the end. You would have a little extra to spend on Angelica, I could earn some extra cash for expenses, and Assistant could buy some new sandals. I know I've been rambling on, but I think it might work. I've been working hard at the music for weeks now and I think I'm ready."

Hermano took his turn: "Billy, everyone in the park knows you were running from something for the long time. Why do you think that we never asked you about what happened back home? We were waiting for you. What took you so long, amigo?"

Billy couldn't speak.

Hermano continued. "You know something?" he asked rhetorically, with a smile spreading across his chubby face, "I think you have the eye for business! I am proud of you! I think I am the good teacher! I see many dinners in the future! Can you begin the music tomorrow night?"

Taking a Breath

After watering his cacti the next morning, Billy decided to wander awhile. He needed some time to straighten his thoughts out. Just a little time for comforting routine. He needed routine.

The fledgling troubadour soon found himself resting on his personal boulder on the breakwall of the Hotel Rosita. Facing south along the bay, he watched the fishermen mending their nets and the pelicans begging for handouts. Small brown crabs darted between crevasses in the breakwall. Dogs roamed the beach — purposefully, with no real purpose.

Billy Emmerson thought of Ruby.

Rising from his perch, he set out back toward his home. There was work to be done before the sun set. Songs had to be rehearsed and the old Martin had to be in perfect tune.

Tick-Tock, Tick-Tock

By the time Billy arrived at Hidalgo that night, several couples and groups of people were already beginning to assemble within its confines. He inhaled deeply of the familiar smells, felt the warm breath of the Pacific upon his face, and adjusted his eyes to the glow of the gargoyle street lights and strings of bulbs defining each merchant's realm. This was a magical place, a world of dreams and hopes. Sometimes, even wishes came true.

As he approached the souvenir stand, he quickly became aware of some dramatic changes that had taken place over the past twenty-four hours.

Both Hermonos were adorned in their best finery. Hermano, the elder, sported carefully creased white slacks and a print shirt depicting lime green palm trees set on a background of purple and pink. Not to be outdone by his mentor, Hermano, the younger, was ablaze in orange trousers accentuated by a multi-colored striped belt tightly drawn around his slim waist. A loose cotton T-shirt of faded yellow proclaimed a direct prayer in bold red letters: "Bring More Tourists to Puerto Vallarta!"

Dressed in his faded cut-offs and simple white tank top, Billy could never hope to rival the sartorial splendour of his friends.

A small wooden stool had been positioned to the left of the shop facing Ordaz. In front of the stool, a glass bowl had been situated directly confronting the attention of passersby. Attached to the bowl with masking tape, was a simple cardboard sign printed in black marker. Two words clarified the sign's intention, one printed in Spanish, and below, another in English: "Propinas," and "Tips."

As Billy placed his guitar case down in front of the stool, he greeted both confidants: *Buenos noches, amigos!* Looks like a good night for business!"

The three stood in front of the stand shaking hands and grinning broadly before anyone spoke.

It was Hermano who broke the silence with staccato-like verbal jabs. "I also think the night will be good! Do you much admire our shirts? Is the stool high enough for you? The glass bowl belongs to the assistant. It was once a house for his fish. It is now sadly departed. Perhaps I will bring Angelica here later. She is the lover of the music! She is also the lover of the strawberry crêpes. She is my angel! At what time do you feel you could make the music?"

Assistant remained silent, but involuntarily bobbed his head to the rhythm of his employer's bombastic beat.

Hermano continued. "Is the guitar adequate enough for you, Billy? I know it is very old. It looks like the park is beginning to fill. Should you begin now?"

"Hold on, amigo!" exclaimed Billy. "Everything looks great! You two look handsome enough to break the hearts of every señorita in Hidalgo. The guitar is fine. It's been a long time, but I'm ready. Let's do a little business first and see what happens."

By nine o'clock that night, the park was bustling. Billy and Assistant were kept busy peddling everything from stuffed frogs to miniature sombreros. Even Hermano had not deserted his post.

Several people, over the last two hours, had inquired about the prominently displayed glass bowl. The portly proprietor's response was always the same: "Come back later. Tonight, Hidalgo will be treated to the music of my good friend, Billy Emmerson from The United States of America!"

By nine-thirty, Hermano could contain himself no longer. "Billy, it is now time to play the songs! We have made many pesos tonight already! I am going to bring my Angelica back here, and, on the way, we will relieve Paco from his business so he will have the great opportunity to hear the music you have made. Okay, amigo?"

"Okay, amigo," replied Billy after pausing briefly. "Just give me a minute to pick up a six-pack and tell Paco you're coming. A person tends to get thirsty playing songs."

It's Showtime!

You're never gonna get wet,
If you never feel the rain,
And you're never gonna be hurt,
If you never feel the pain,
And if that's what you want,
I wish you all the best.
I hope you meet with happiness.
I hope you find success,
But if you don't learn the steps,
And never take a chance,
You'll never hear the music,
And you'll never learn to dance.

-Snake Adams, 1978

By ten, Hermano had returned with Paco and Angelica.

Hermano's angel had gained considerable heft since Billy had last seen her, but tonight she looked almost radiant. In keeping with her spouse's festive apparel, Angelica was draped in a form-concealing, long white smock, decorated with two stylized pink flamingos. Each flamingo was strategically placed over one of Angelica's ample breasts. Each bird gazed upward with an open beak. If one were to ignore the strawberry stains spattered directly above the flamingos' gaping bills, Angelica evoked a picture of heavenly rapture.

Paco had abandoned his corner store with

little urging from Hermano. He had left his wife in charge. He had temporarily escaped his clerical and marital responsibilities. Paco appeared in excellent spirits. The plastic bag he carried in his left hand, did little to conceal the six-pack of cold Mexican libations intended to elevate his mood even higher. Billy had become somewhat of a fixture in Paco's life. He enjoyed living vicariously through Billy's stories. Paco looked forward to witnessing his friend's performance.

A group of around thirty tourists and local people had congregated around the stand by this time in collective anticipation of the forthcoming event.

The time seemed right to Billy. His friends had gathered. Familiar faces abounded. No Mrs. Blue-Hair people in sight.

The Martin was tuned. He was sure of the songs.

As Billy positioned himself comfortably on the stool, he reached for a cold can of Modelo and quaffed deeply. Placing the half-drained container to a readily accessible location on his right, he withdrew the old Martin from its case and cradled it gently on his lap.

A chord was struck and the musician began.

Relying on the familiar, Billy broke into the first verse of his one-man rendition of "Hard Driven Rain." Strumming in a moderately up-beat tempo, he delivered the lyrics in a confident raspy tone befitting incessant winds and bone-chilling downpours. As the last note disappeared into eternity, Billy Emmerson braced himself and waited for the verdict. What followed was the dreaded pause that every musician feared. It didn't last long. It was not born of apathy, but of highly exceeded expectations. Applause erupted, suddenly shattering the silence. The outpouring was unrestrained and enthusiastic. It was loud and sustained.

Billy thanked the crowd and smiled gratefully.

Hermano continued to clap, Assistant whistled, and Paco raised a can to salute his friend. Angelica grinned so unabashedly, her silver-rimmed teeth shone like ethereal stars.

For his next selection, Billy chose a new song he had written with fondness and joy — "Ruby in the Sun." The piece was bright and spoke of simple times spent in enjoying simple pleasures. Again, the applause was intense.

The young performer was elated! For Billy, this was better than any concert at which he had ever played. The people were simply enjoying the music he had created. There was no hype, elaborate arrangements, fancy staging, blinding spotlights or trendy sound effects. It was Billy Emmerson and an old Martin acoustic guitar.

Thank you, God for this moment, he thought. Billy was a devout agnostic. He could curse or pray, depending on circumstances.

The music continued for the next hour. A few Squires' tunes were combined with recent originals such as "Lost in the Jungle," "Fish

Net," and "Too Much Tequila" to round out a performance that was an unqualified success. Every song met with unconstrained applause and cheering.

When Billy had exhausted his repertoire for the evening, everyone in the park agreed he had taken part in something very special.

Thanking his audience in both English and passable Spanish, the balladeer promised to play again soon.

As the crowd began to dissipate, Hermano and Assistant rushed to Billy with congratulations and pats on the back. Paco hiccupped as he wove his way homeward and proclaimed the evening, "a most excellent fiesta!" Angelica's teeth reflected her open-mouthed appreciation.

"Look, Billy," exclaimed a bubbling Hermano, "the fish house is crowded with the pesos and American dollars! Let us load the truck with our merchandise and money and celebrate! You have only sipped of your beer. Tonight, I will buy you many! Come, Angelica, my dove!" continued the Mexican jumping bean, "You can help also. The late dinner of your choice will be your reward!"

That night, the cart was bedded down hastily and the old pickup was loaded in record time.

The waiters at La Scala more than earned their generous tips that evening. Great quantities of garlic shrimp and buttered lobster tails were consumed by the quartet of revellers, and tray after tray of cold *cerveza* and Cokes were delivered as soon as the last had been poured down parched throats.

As the celebration drew to a close, Hermano proposed a toast to the evening's success and declared the next night a holiday for all.

Billy and his guitar somehow navigated the cobblestones to the sanctity of home.

As Billy crawled under his Mexican blanket that night, he was emotionally drained. He was excited, yet grateful for the sleep he knew would be momentarily forthcoming. He wanted to dream in technicolor.

Enter, Rutherford
or
William's New Lodger

The following day was one of rest for Hidalgo's new celebrity. After taking his time over his traditional two cups of thick Mexican *café clásico*, and examining the bent old tamarind on the boulevard for visible signs of aging, Billy retreated to the beach. It was already midmorning, as he had slept later than usual, and the sun had already begun its relentless climb to its zenith.

As he lumbered down onto his sun-baked boulder on the breakwall of the Hotel Rosita, Billy took great solace in the fact that his world seemed eternally constant. He understood that he required routine and consistency. He knew that this need for order sometimes bordered on the obsessive. Conversely, he realized that this internal exigency did nothing to damage the happiness of a single soul, including his own. He liked things the way they were but, could still take a chance with the best of 'em.

Keep the movie on hold.

Fat, mottled sea birds continued their supportive relationship with weathered brown fishermen. Emaciated stray dogs still roamed the sand in quest of lost morsels of sustenance. Local children kicked a soccer ball between goal posts of sun-dried coconut shells.

At mid-day, Billy began to grow restless. As

he stretched and decided to move on, a familiar sight came into view. Approaching along the beach from the north, and cutting through the fishing community, a young man, carrying a large green iguana on his shoulder and a camera in his hand, approached Billy within speaking distance. Billy had often seen the youth patrolling local beaches engaged in his own unique way of earning a living. For several pesos, tourists could purchase a photograph of themselves sporting the placid reptile in various contrived positions. The picture made for an interesting tale over drinks with friends, when the vacationers' trip was over.

Billy had heard the teenager speak in impeccable English when reeling in potential customers, so he knew communication would not be a problem as the two engaged in greeting.

"Hola, amigo!" Billy began with a smile. "How's it goin' today?"

"Not so bad, but I think today will be my last day on the beach." The young photographer seemed despondent and replied to Billy's question with downcast eyes.

"Why? What's the matter?" pursued Billy.

"My cousin found me a really good hotel job in Cancun and I have to report to work in two days."

"Isn't that good news?"

"Yeah, but what will I do with Fluffy? I can't take him along."

Billy could see how the boy and Fluffy were so

lovingly attached by the way the young man scratched the lizard's spiked back while making soothing clicking sounds of endearment directed at his companion.

"Couldn't you just sell him?" inquired Billy.

"Maybe, but how could I be sure he'd have a good home? I don't want him living just anywhere."

Jesus! thought Billy, *That reptile reminds me of my Uncle Rutherford! Same saggy turkey neck. Same little beady eyes. They could be twins!*

Billy continued: "What does he eat? Is he hard to look after? Does he need some kind of cage?"

"No. He's no problema. He eats vegetables and fruit. He loves bananas! I have a cage, but he never uses it. Why do you ask?"

"Well, I haven't had a pet since my cat, Squinty went to animal heaven about twenty years ago, and this lizard of yours reminds me of my favorite uncle from back home. Let's talk, amigo."

Five minutes later a deal was struck and Billy became the proud owner of a two-foot iguana named Fluffy.

On the way back home to Hallowe'en Street, Billy found himself glancing at the iguana perched on his shoulder after every few steps.

"I can't believe how much you look like my uncle," he uttered while addressing his new amigo.

"Would you consider a name change?"

Fluffy blinked.

Billy interpreted the gesture as a sign of assent.

"Okay, boy, from now on, I'm calling you Rutherford!"

The remainder of the day was devoted to the care and feeding of tropical, green creatures.

After dropping Rutherford off at home with a dish of water and instructions to behave himself, Billy's first stop was the local mini-grocery about three blocks from the apartment. Here, he purchased a bag of frozen mixed vegetables and a bunch of ripe bananas. Nothing too good for Rutherford.

Next, on Billy's agenda, was the Woolworth department store situated a block west of Hallowe'en Street. Here, he procured a blue dog dish, a small foam pillow, and a set of large plastic children's building blocks.

As Billy climbed the steps leading into his home, he felt certain his roommate would be pleased with his gifts.

Setting the bags down, he unlocked the door, placed the items down just inside the apartment, and closed the door behind him.

"I'm home, Rutherford! Wait 'til you see what I've got for you! Rutherford?"

As Billy began a cursory hunt around his home, he began to worry. Rutherford was nowhere in sight.

"Rutherford, where the hell are you? You come out right now or I'll eat the bananas!"

Billy's threat fell on whatever passed for the iguana's deaf ears.

The search continued. This time, in-depth. After probing and peering into every conceivable hiding place, options were becoming almost nonexistent. Carefully pulling out the old refrigerator from the wall, and sinking to his knees to better examine this final refuge, Billy was both relieved and annoyed to discover Rutherford dozing blissfully in his newly-discovered haven.

Dragging his pet gently from his hiding place, Billy swore he saw a sheepish grin spread across Rutherford's face.

"Jeez, boy, is this what it's gonna be like living with you? At least Lizzy never crawled behind the fridge! But, to be fair though, you don't talk as much as she did. Come on, I'm gonna build you a new house!"

Placing the pillow on the floor in the corner of the kitchen, Billy began construction of the walls, following the outside dimensions of the lizard mattress. The walls were soon completed, and an archaic, deeply worn cutting board from the kitchen was appropriated to serve as a makeshift roof.

"Perfect!" proclaimed Billy. "Now, let's see how you like your new *casa*!"

Rutherford seemed delighted. After being placed ceremoniously in his new home, he craned his scaly head, examined his new surroundings, closed his eyes, and immediately drifted off into a deep iguana slumber.

"This is better," Billy whispered, proud of his own handiwork and thankful that Rutherford felt comfortable. "Now, I'll get to work."

Several hours later, Billy propped his guitar against the living room wall, put his pen down, and began to prepare dinner. Cheeseburgers seemed in order.

Billy and Rutherford dined together that evening. As the man finished his second ketchup-laden *hamburguesa*, the reptile cleaned his own bowl of the last bites of vegetables and cubed bananas.

"What would you like to do now, boy? How about a little walk?"

As the two departed, it was Rutherford who most seemed to look forward to their evening stroll. He had a new home, a full belly, and someone to carry him about — certainly much better than foraging for himself somewhere along the banks of the Rio Cuale.

Carefully weaving their way up and down the Malecón that evening, the pair turned the heads of every passerby — a sun-stained gringo and his emerald companion out for a leisurely promenade. The city had embraced Elizabeth Taylor and Richard Burton decades earlier. Now it had Billy Emmerson and Rutherford.

Later that night, as the two settled into their beds, Billy worked out chord changes for a new song in his mind before drifting off. Rutherford contemplated ripe bananas for breakfast.

Back on the Line

When Billy awoke the next morning and opened his eyes, he was startled, yet somehow not totally surprised at the first image he encountered for the new day. Facing him on the pillow was Rutherford. Because of their close proximity, Billy could smell sour bananas on the lizard's breath. It was not the most pleasant panorama the young musician had ever pictured upon awakening. *God,* he thought, *at least Lizzy never smelled like bananas when she gained consciousness!*

For the remainder of the day, Billy worked on new songs. Chord progressions were finalized and lyrics were polished. Rutherford ate and napped. It seemed like a relationship with which they both could live.

By nightfall, Billy was anxious to resume his responsibilities in the park. It had been an interesting holiday, but he was eager to return to the bustle of Hidalgo.

Making sure that Rutherford's bowl was filled with delicacies, the *norteamericano* soon found himself back on familiar concrete.

"Hey, Hermano! Good to see you! How're you doing tonight?"

"I'm good, my friend. How about you? Did you have the good rest yesterday?"

"Yeah, it was good. I'll tell you about it later. It was fun. Did you get to spend some time with Angelica?"

"Si! We also had the good time! After she

finished her work at the *farmacia,* we went back to La Scala for another dinner. We talked much about your music. She loves the songs very much! She also loves the spaghetti and meat balls!"

At this point, Billy glanced over to Assistant who was already completing his first sale of the evening. As the young Hermano accepted payment for three hand-painted ceramic thimbles, he met his partner's eyes, smiled, and shook his head slightly. Billy expected and understood the subtle, habitual gesture.

The exuberant, elder of the Hermanos continued: "Billy, I have something for you!" Reaching into his pocket, he withdrew several pesos and handed them over to his employee. "In American money, this sum comes to nearly twelve dollars! This is good payment for the singing of the songs. Are you most certain that the helper and I should be included in the sharing of profit? We did nothing to earn our percentage."

"Thanks, boss. It is a lot of money for just singing a few songs. You got the Martin for me and Assistant donated the fish house. I appreciate everything. We're partners aren't we?"

Hermano was visibly touched, but not so overwhelmed with sentiment that he couldn't inquire: "So when do you think you might play again, Billy?"

Billy laughed. "Soon, amigo, but I have a lot

of work to do first. Let's sell some stuff tonight. Assistant's sandals look pretty ragged!"

The night's labors proved lucrative. Trinkets were sold, Hermano managed to slip off into the open arms of his true love, and Billy Emmerson received more than his share of inviting glances from pretty señoritas who had heard him perform two nights previously.

When the shift came to a close, Billy was eager to get home, snap open a tab of his favorite brew, and examine the damage he was certain Rutherford had inflicted upon his humble dwelling.

He was wrong. Not only did everything appear in order, but Rutherford was snoozing peacefully in the *mini-casa* Billy had fabricated for him. Draining his second can of Modelo, the new landlord undressed and pulled back the blanket on his bed, anticipating a good night's sleep. Crawling under the covering, he was unexpectedly surprised at Rutherford's attempt to repay his master's ongoing generosity. Wiping the sticky smear from his shoulder, Billy included Rutherford in his prayers: "Jesus, I hope I can litter train the little bugger!"

Fairly Confident

Keep on laughing. Life's a joke.
Grab the ring and go for broke!
At the end of the ride,
You can raise your glass,
And tell them all to kiss your ass!

-Doolie and The Demolishers, 1973

Over the next two weeks, Billy divided his time between work and pleasure. Nights in the park continued to be productive and joyful. Days spent writing fresh lyrics and composing new music proved invigorating, yet at times, exhausting. The care and feeding of Rutherford fell somewhere in between.

During a slow period in sales one night, Hermano casually brought up the subject of the next public performance of Billy Emmerson from America. "Billy, do you think you have enough songs to once again make the music?"

"I think so, my friend. I've been busy writing, and most of the tunes are pretty good. At least I hope so."

"Then, let's do it tomorrow! It will be *fantástico!*" Hermano's enthusiasm was contagious.

Even the characteristically reticent Assistant could not contain himself. "*Firstary*, I clean my house of fish!"

I think I'd better spend more time with his

English lessons, thought Billy.

Speaking aloud, a simple "Okay," was all that was required to consolidate the next evening's festivities.

Playing and Playmates

When Billy arrived at the park the next evening, the re-born singer felt much more confident in his abilities than he did at the onset of his initial presentation. The Martin was fine-tuned and polished. Billy now had enough new material to present before a live audience.

Hermano and his young associate had once again set up the stool and the fish bowl to the left of the stand. New light bulbs had replaced the dead.

"Buenas noches, Billy!" exclaimed an exalted Hermano as the two shook hands.

"Hey, boss! What's happening?" returned Vallarta's new patriot.

"Just waiting for you. Do you want to begin the music now?"

"Maybe not quite yet! We should peddle some of our wares first and start when it feels right. Thanks for setting everything up though. It looks really good."

"De nada, but it was the *muchacho* who did the up setting."

Entering, as if on cue, the young novice approached the cart from the general vicinity of the public washrooms located toward the back of the park. Upon first glance, Billy knew the teenager must have been primping in front of the restroom's small cloudy mirror.

The effect was disarming. Tonight, Assistant had donned a spotless white dress shirt accessorized with a wide red tie depicting the face of a smiling Bugs Bunny. The words, "What's up, Doc?" ballooned over the rabbit's buck-toothed grin. Assistant's sharply creased, black dress pants dragged to the ground and covered his sandals.

"Wow, man! You look really spiffy! Is your girlfriend coming tonight or something? You look like something out of a magazine!" Billy joked.

Assistant didn't quite grasp the intended humour. "Gracias, Billy," answered the foppish dandy. "Yes, she is. I tell her I am the one to look after things. I tell her I be a big friend of the American rolling and rocking star. Is okay?"

"Sure, it's okay, buddy! You can tell her you're my agent if you want!" Billy had no idea that a girlfriend existed before Assistant's confession, but if he could somehow help his friend down the road to romance, he would certainly do his best. Billy continued: "Back in the States, I had a manager. He was a good guy, but you're a much sharper dresser!"

"Gracias again, Billy." Assistant lowered his head in gratitude and took his place behind the counter.

What the hell, thought Billy, *I'll dedicate a song to her tonight from her handsome boyfriend. That should score him some points.*

After a couple of hours, it was time for the concert to begin. It felt right. Familiar faces had been gathering around the stand for the last half hour expecting to see a repeat performance. Billy was pleased that word of mouth, a fish bowl, and a stool could attract such interest. Back in Illinois, promotion was much more complicated.

The lovely Angelica clung to the protective arm of her well-nourished knight as they both chomped on hot buttered ears of corn purchased at a nearby food stand. Even the particles of hastily chewed kernels adhering to her chin didn't seem to diminish Hermano's open admiration for his divine inspiration. It showed in his eyes.

Paco was also in attendance. This time, a small brown paper bag, outlining the shape of a bottle, had replaced the six-pack he had carried the last time. *Paco's becoming quite the party animal,* thought Billy.

Assistant had disappeared some time ago, and Billy wondered to where his new "agent" had made such a surreptitious retreat. The answer was immediately forthcoming. Approaching the souvenir stand from the general direction of Calle Venezuela, Billy observed a beaming Assistant shuffling arm-in-arm with a very pretty, very young señorita. She was petite in stature, but her high heels and long legs made her appear several inches taller. Ink-black hair, cut two or three inches above her shoulder, framed a pixie-like face. Fair complexion. Large, doe-like brown eyes. She was dressed in a plain white T-shirt and a very brief denim skirt.

Man, thought Billy, *if I were ten years*

younger...

"Hola, Billy!" exclaimed Assistant, with self-assurance, as the pair neared within greeting distance. "This is *mi amiga*, Maria."

"Hola, Maria. Glad to meet a friend of Hermano. I hope you like the songs tonight. Hermano has helped me a great deal."

"I'm sure I will," replied Maria in heavily accented English. "Hermano has told me much about you. He has helped me in many ways also."

Don't even go there, Billy commanded himself.

The guitarist's second performance in Hidalgo was even more exhilarating than his debut. Several new songs were introduced, and judging from the enthusiastic reaction of the audience, everyone seemed to enjoy the tunes immensely.

At one point, during one of the more up-tempo melodies, Hermano, the proprietor, and his beloved angel were captivated by the rhythm and broke into spontaneous dance! The onlookers cleared a space so the couple could express themselves with more freedom. Paco clapped loudly to the beat. Assistant turned to Maria and grinned sheepishly.

While Angelica chose to remain fairly stationary, juggling her rotund torso and flailing her meaty arms in syncopation, Hermano assumed a completely different mode of locomotion. Prancing around his love like a force-fed bantam rooster about to mate, he bobbed his head, shook his hands, and twisted his short legs into impossible contortions. Sometimes, he would face his partner. Sometimes he would circle to the rear and move in unison with Angelica's bouncing buttocks. The entire park seemed to be clapping in time and cheering approvingly at the gyrations of the happy couple. Billy, not wishing the show to end, repeated two verses and extended the final chorus before closing. The crowd burst into shouts and whistles of approval!

Hermano gently took Angelica's hand into his own and bent before her on one knee. Sensing something important was about to ensue, the assembly grew silent with anticipation.

Gazing up into Angelica's loving eyes, Hermano chose his words carefully. Roughly translated, Billy took them to mean: "I love you, Angelica. For a woman of your fine proportions, you dance like a scorpion in a hot frying pan!"

Again, people applauded wildly!

Maria shrugged.

Billy took a break.

A couple of hours later, after performing and hawking Mexican keepsakes between sets, a tired, but gratified Billy Emmerson gently placed his old Martin in its worn case. It had been a very successful evening. The fish bowl was brimming with coins and small denominations of paper currency. Maria had pitched in and sold more than her share of baubles. Assistant gleamed with elation, Hermano with avarice, and Billy, with a sense of accomplishment.

As the musician was about to snap his guitar case shut, he noticed one of the three young *mariachis* who had been listening intently to his songs over the past hour approach tentatively and offer an outstretched hand. A Spanish guitar was strapped to his back.

"Pardon me, señor," the stranger began. "My name is Pedro Briones. I play guitar with my two friends over there in our travelling band."

Billy shook the man's hand, smiled, and nodded toward the remaining two group members who had lingered several steps behind.

"Buenas noches, amigo. Mi llamo, Billy Emmerson."

Pedro continued. "We have been listening to your music and enjoy it very much. We admire American rock 'n' roll even when it is played on one guitar."

"Thank you, Pedro. I appreciate the compliment," Billy replied with sincerity.

"May I introduce you to my friends?" The young Mexican gestured, and he and Billy were joined by the two other *mariachis.*

Both were dressed identically to Pedro in white slacks and matching cotton shirts. Bright red scarfs were tied loosely around each member's neck. The taller of the two carried a large acoustic bass guitar cradled in his arms, while the other displayed a glistening chrome snare drum attached around his neck with a thick yellow cord. Drum sticks stuck out of his left hand.

Handshakes were performed and names were exchanged. The bass player was Juan Flores from San Blas. The drummer simply introduced himself as Clint.

"Is Clint your real name?" inquired Billy unable to suppress a smile.

"Si , amigo. It's a long story. Let us just say that my father very much enjoys American films of the west. I do as well."

"Is that how you learned to speak English so well?" asked Billy.

"No," answered the drummer. "All of us learned from a wonderful teacher. Television!"

The four laughed.

Pedro resumed: "Do you think we could buy you a beer and talk about music for awhile?"

"I really don't know," answered Billy. "I'd have to ask my boss. I usually help him pack up this stuff after work."

Hermano was in too good a mood to deny the request. "Go ahead, my friend! There are many hands for helping tonight!"

It was Pedro's idea that the four traverse one of the side streets off Ordaz and sit down for a few cold ones in a quiet café frequented by patrons from the immediate neighborhood.

Instruments were put aside. Beer was ordered. Beer was consumed. Musical trends were discussed — sometimes with gravity, most often, with levity.

Soon, the small table around which the foursome sat had become laden with empty bottles. Tongues were beginning to loosen. Juan from San Blas spoke up in a low but confident voice: "We have heard your music tonight, Billy. We like it very much. What we do is different. We travel from one restaurant to the other singing Mexican songs we hope the tourists will like. If they like the songs, they pay us. Sometimes they take our picture. It's okay, but it's not what we really want to do. Would you like to come to my place tomorrow and hear us play what we really like?"

"Yeah, I sure would!" answered Billy, somewhat surprised at the quickness of his response. "Give me the time and directions and I'll be there!"

One more round was ordered and disposed of in rapid time. The four new friends parted company until the morrow. Billy noticed that Clint exited dramatically, in a slow, John Wayne rolling stride.

As he neared Hallowe'en Street, and began his ascent, a picture of Rutherford flashed through Billy's mind and broke the spell of a perfect night. *I hope the little leech is sleeping in his own bed.*

He wasn't.

Big John and the Boys

The next day, at around two, Billy found himself knocking at the entrance of a modest first story apartment on 5 de Febrero, a side street just across the Rio Cuale.

The wooden door swung open almost immediately and the young musician from Chicago was met by the young *mariachi* from San Blas.

"*Buenas tardes,* Billy! Come on in."

"Gracias, Juan. Good to see you."

Upon entering, Billy was greeted by Pedro and Clint in typical Mexican-fashion handshakes and polite salutations.

"How do you like my apartment?" inquired Juan with a sweeping gesture of his hand.

"Jesus!" exclaimed Billy, while surveying his host's surroundings with open wonder.

Spread along the front of the entire living room wall were two massive Traynor amplifiers flanking a complete set of Ludwig drums. Two microphones, mounted on stands, were positioned in front of the equipment. Several guitars, including a Fender electric and a Rickenbacker bass were scattered around the room, either placed on stands or propped against chairs.

"This is amazing! Where did you guys get all this heavy duty stuff?" Billy was awestruck.

Clint answered for the group: "Sometimes, rich Americans *really* like Mexican songs, especially if they've had too many tequilas! Drunken gringos are the best! No offence, Billy."

"None taken, amigo, but what kind of music do you play with all this equipment?" asked Billy, gradually beginning to adjust to the scene.

"We can show you if you like," replied Juan. "I'm not saying that we're great or anything, but I don't think we're too bad."

As if on cue, Pedro picked up the Fender, flicked on an amplifier, and positioned himself behind a mic. Juan followed suit, except his instrument of choice was the Rickenbacker bass. By this time, Clint had poised himself behind the drums with sticks in hand.

Pedro glanced at Juan and smiled. He nodded at Clint. Clint nodded back.

"Two-three-four!" shouted the drummer.

The song began. It was loud. It was raw. It was rock 'n' roll, the way it was meant to be played. "Mustang Sally" never sounded so good!

When Clint crashed his cymbal, accenting the final beat, all three musicians scanned Billy's face, hoping for a positive reaction.

"Man, you guys are good! Where did you learn to play like that? Don't tell me television!" Billy reacted in a state of disbelief. It had been a long time since he had heard anything like this.

Pedro answered Billy's question. "We learned from records. Wanna jam, amigo?"

"Can I borrow a guitar?" Billy needed no encouragement.

The session lasted several hours. It was

gruelling, and at times, frustrating. There were times when Billy's fingers failed to respond as quickly as they should have to his mental commands. There were times when he had difficulty hitting the high notes when he was expected to. There were times when he missed a shift in tempo. It was the best jam session in which he had ever participated!

When the amplifiers were finally deadened, Juan made a much appreciated offer. "You guys wanna come into the kitchen and have some beer?"

"Sounds good!" returned Billy. Pedro and Clint acquiesced.

Today was Sunday, Billy's night off from his duties in Hidalgo. Besides, he was having too much fun to go home now. He had to come down from his high gradually.

The quartet adjourned to a small kitchen off of Juan's living area and gratefully began to enjoy clear, frosty bottles of Corona which had been distributed by their munificent host.

Pedro was the first to broach the topic of music. "So, what do you think, Billy? How did you like playing with us?"

"I haven't had this much fun in a long time," replied the American with a trace of repressed self-indulgence creeping into his words. "It's good once in awhile in the park, but it's a lot better playing with guys like you. I really miss it."

"Did you play in a band or something?"

asked Clint.

"Yeah, I did, but it seems like it was in another life. Some of the songs you heard in the park were from the old days. Another guy and myself used to write some pretty good songs together."

Juan plunked down some more *cerveza*.

Billy began to unwind. He continued. "I was in a band in the States, in Chicago. We were pretty good. Even had a record out."

"What were you called?" inquired Juan.

"The Chicago Squires."

"Never heard of you," replied Juan from San Blas, with complete innocence.

Billy laughed and responded: "Yeah, well we weren't The Beatles or anything, but that single we had out hit number three! That's not too shabby, amigos!"

"What was it called?" It was Pedro's turn to ask a question.

"Hard Driven Rain," Billy replied with a hint of arrogance. He glanced at the bass player to gauge his reaction.

Juan from San Blas met Billy's eyes and replied indifferently, "Never heard of it."

"Shit!" was the ex-Squire's reaction.

The night continued. A few more details were added to Billy's story. Much was revealed about the *mariachis'* history and future aspirations.

After tipping back several more cold Coronas, Billy decided it was time to begin his trek back to Hallowe'en Street. The journey could be tricky if he drank any more beer.

Shaking hands with his new friends at the door, Billy thanked each one, and prepared to depart.

"Wanna do this again, amigo?" asked Pedro. His eyes, rivetted to Billy's, seemed to demand more than a simple response. Billy understood.

"Thought you'd never ask, man! My days are free. Just let me know and I'll be here!"

Smiling as though some secret pact had been signed, Pedro added: "Billy, would you do me a favor, amigo?"

"Sure."

"Would you call me, 'Pete' please?"

"Sure."

Juan was next. "Billy, would 'John' be alright?"

"Sure."

Clint looked bewildered and hesitant, but finally asked: "Umm...would it be okay if you called me...Clint?"

"Sure."

Life Goes On

It's the end of the night,
And the music has stopped,
And you're tired and thinking of bed,
But you know you won't sleep,
'Cause you still feel the beat,
Of a rock 'n' roll song,
In your head.

-Tie Buchanan, 1969

When Billy arrived at the park Monday evening, he was surprised to see Maria, once again, helping Assistant perform his designated duties. Dressed in her short denim skirt, she was stretching to adjust the lights framing the shop's awning. She was stretching very high.

Jesus! Billy exclaimed to himself.

His licentious images were immediately shattered by Assistant's voice. "Hola, my friend! Is okay Maria helps us tonight? The big boss is once again with his Angelica. He left when the truck was empty. I believe that Angelica's belly may also be empty."

"Sure, it's okay, partner!" Although Billy didn't want to sound *too* enthusiastic, he couldn't help notice a coquettish smile appear on Maria's face as she pretended not to hear.

"*Bueno!*" proclaimed Assistant. "Let's sell some shit!"

This kid's English is starting to improve!

thought Billy with a certain amount of pride.

Throughout the shift, the trio sold enough bangles to make Hermano proud. Without question, the allure of having Maria present bolstered business dramatically.

Billy recounted his adventure with Pete, John, and Clint to the young Assistant who seemed genuinely pleased that his friend had enjoyed himself so much. "Will you do it again?" he asked Billy.

"I sure hope so. Pete said he'd let me know soon."

"Maybe I could go with you sometime."

"Maybe. I don't see why not, but let me check first," Billy replied conditionally.

"That would be so cool, man!" exclaimed Assistant excitedly.

Where's he learning this stuff? pondered Billy.

The once reticent Assistant also had tales to tell his shop-mate tonight. Whenever Maria was busy with customers, he would slyly serve up a tasty tidbit to his American friend.

"I first met her on the Malecón." Assistant beamed with bliss. Billy nodded encouragingly. Business would beckon, and Assistant would find himself preoccupied for several moments before the story resumed.

"I've also attended the cinema with her."

"Good!" *What else?* thought Billy.

Customers would call upon Assistant's services and he would once more disappear.

Often, Billy would be required to deal with English speaking souvenir hunters and the story was once again halted abruptly.

By the end of the night, Billy had learned very little. He was certain however that young Hermano was one very lucky *hombre.*

At eleven-thirty, Hermano arrived in his old pickup and the four began to pack up the tools of their trade.

"You have a good time tonight, my friend?" inquired Billy as he and Hermano carefully shifted merchandise in the truck's bed.

"Oh, si!" exclaimed the bubbly businessman. "We ate much and also went to the dance at Los Tortugas Bar and Grill!"

"Tomorrow though," he continued, "Angelica must work late at her store so I will be with you to demonstrate the experience!"

Actually, thought Billy, *we seem to do okay by ourselves.*

To Hermano, he answered, "That's good news, boss! Things just aren't the same when you're gone."

Hermano's chest swelled with gratification. His belly swelled with tacos.

"How did Maria handle the work tonight?" he asked as she and Assistant were occupied wrapping coffee cups in newspaper back at the stand.

"She was fine," stated Billy honestly. "She's very good with the younger people. They all enjoy dealing with her, especially the boys."

"Good! If the business continues to prosper, perhaps she might work more for us." Hermano jabbed his cheek.

When the truck was loaded and the mobile hut was put to rest for the night, Billy bade his friends good-night and headed up Octubre to his apartment.

Entering his living room a few moments later, he was surprised to see Rutherford sleeping soundly in his own bed. "Jesus," Billy said quietly to himself, so as not to awaken the iguana, "maybe he's learning after all."

After indulging in a cold beer and preparing himself for sleep, the young merchant-musician climbed into his rumpled bed and pulled up his Mexican blanket.

"Shit! Damn you, lizard!" This time, Billy was not worried about awakening his boarder.

Rutherford had left his master another gift.

Busy, Busy, Busy

The next morning, although Billy was tempted to call upon John, he relinquished the thought and decided instead to begin the day slowly and routinely.

Studying the fishing community while balanced upon his personal boulder never failed to intrigue the young man. Billy never tired of the picture: sun-baked elders repairing nets, muscular younger men setting out to test their skill against the Pacific, and clumsy pelicans scavenging breakfast.

Besides, he often recalled warm memories of Ruby as he sat in the sun and let his mind wander. Billy Emmerson missed her dearly, but realized he had never loved her in the way he had always imagined it would be. He had never really experienced the feeling, but was hopeful he would recognize it, if it ever came along — something about dragons and damsels in distress.

Billy's musings ceased when he realized how high the sun had climbed.

There were other matters to which he must attend. Important matters. Although he lived in paradise, Billy was not the kind of man to shirk his responsibilities. Today, he had to water his cacti, clean some dishes, sweep the kitchen floor and buy some instant coffee! He figured he could complete these tasks in about fifteen minutes. That would still leave time for beach combing and street wandering before he had to report to work.

I shouldn't push myself so hard, Billy thought with a grin. *After all, I'm on Mexican time! Mañana...*

An Invitation

That night, about an hour after the sun had plunged into the waters of Bandaras Bay, Mr. Emmerson, formerly of Chicago, was visited at his place of employment by Mr. Flores, formerly of San Blas.

Billy was pleased that after John had been introduced to his friends and business associates, they had seemed to take an instant liking to the *mariachi*. Almost immediately, a lively conversation in Spanish erupted, accented with spurts of laughter and spirited gesturing toward Billy. At one point, Hermano strummed an imaginary guitar and sang a few lines of "Hard Driven Rain" in English. He actually possessed a strong baritone voice which somehow seemed incongruous with the body from which it sprang.

Apparently, John had familiarized Hermano, Maria and Assistant with the jam session in which Billy had participated. Billy surmised that Hermano, not to be outdone in the art of story telling, had informed the bass player of his own vast knowledge of Billy's musical prowess.

Although Assistant knew of the session beforehand from Billy, he feigned exaggerated interest and attention throughout John's re-telling. To do otherwise, would have appeared most indecorous.

When the dialogue came to a close, John turned to Billy, switched to English, and asked openly if the ex-Squire could attend another session to be held the next day. There were no qualms about delivering the invitation in front of Billy's friends.

Billy accepted without hesitation and was gratified to see his amigos nodding their heads in approbation.

For some reason however, a trace of guilt flashed through his mind after accepting John's request so readily.

Once John had bid them all farewell and had set out in a southerly direction along the Malecón, Billy decided to assuage his feeling of disloyalty by appealing to Hermano's business sense.

"Hermano," he began, "I was thinking that maybe we could set up the fish house soon and make ourselves a little extra *dinero*. If Maria is going to be around, I wouldn't have to bounce back and forth between music and business. What do you think, boss?" Billy did not want his amigo to think he was being abandoned for new pursuits or friends.

"Fantástico!" exclaimed the felicitous financier while raising his arms skyward. "I bet we make more money than ever before! My sweet angel demands many of the dinners, my friend!"

Billy and Hermano pumped hands and patted each other's shoulders in unrestrained exuberance.

When the ribald ritual between friends gradually subsided, Hermano stepped back and looked up at Billy with eyes that seemed to penetrate the musicians thoughts. He spoke slowly and with great deliberation: "Billy Emmerson...my friend...tomorrow...I want you to play your songs...give them...wings!"

"I will, my friend. I promise."

Making Magic

Outside, it's raining. The wind cuts like a knife.
It's a typical day in her typical life.
With two cups of coffee and a deadline to meet,
She rushes to work with no time to eat.

-The Chicago Squires, 1982

The next day, as Billy wound his way along Ordaz to Febrero, his mind was too pre-occupied to even notice the squawking sales pitches of the troglodytes lurking within niches between store fronts as they gleaned their livelihood promoting tours or extolling the virtues of condominium living. These ravenous, yelping hyenas assaulted each passing tourist with carefully rehearsed lines: "Hey, amigo! Where you from? Great tan! You look Mexican! How long you staying? Where you going for dinner? Free drink for you at this restaurant! Wanna go on a cruise? Wanna rent a jeep? Free breakfast! Just give me a moment of your time." These people could be amusing or very aggravating depending on one's mood. They usually left Billy alone. Today, he was oblivious to their self-aggrandizing rantings.

Billy continued. Not even tourists, who inevitably stopped in the middle of the sidewalk to gawk at something in a storefront window or congregated in obstructive groups to debate over which friend or relative back home would most deserve a specific purchase proved a detriment.

He sidestepped them with alacrity.

Billy was deliberate in his steps.

His mind was focussed on his music.

In the musician's right hand, he carried a plastic bag containing four copies of each of twelve original songs. Seven of the tunes he had written in Vallarta. The remaining five had been composed in Chicago in collaboration with David Hanson. Every song came complete with accompanying guitar chords printed above appropriate phrases or verses.

It took Billy a few minutes to cross the bridge over the Rio Cuale and arrive at John's place.

It took John a few seconds to respond to Billy's knocking.

"Come on in, Billy! Pete and Clint are setting up. How are you doing? Hope you didn't mind me coming to see you at the park last night." The bassist seemed anxious to get to the music.

"I'm good, John. How're you?"

Billy raised a hand to greet Pete and Clint who were engaged in testing microphones and checking sound levels.

To John, Billy continued: "I'm glad you came over to the park last night. My friends really like you. When you left, Hermano, my boss, even encouraged me to show you some of the material I wrote. You probably heard me play some of the songs at the park the other night."

"Sounds good, my friend!" John exclaimed. "Let's see how they're doing with the equipment."

"What's happening, amigos?" inquired Billy as he and John crossed the room and met Pete and Clint.

"Just getting ready to make some noise!" Clint was ready to gallop down rock 'n' roll trails.

"Everything's tuned and ready to go," added Pete. "Use the Strat again if you want. I like how you play it."

"Thanks, Pete," answered Billy. "Maybe we could warm up a bit and I could show you some of my tunes later, if it's okay with you guys."

"We'd like that, *hombre!* Couldn't wait 'til you got here today!" Pete's honesty and enthusiasm were contagious.

Billy couldn't wait to strap on the guitar. Some fifty minutes later, the quartet had loosened up enough to deserve a short break and a cold Corona. Seated around John's small kitchen table, sipping his beer, Billy felt comfortable enough to bring up the topic of his songs.

"You guys wanna see some of my stuff now?" Billy inquired, trying not to seem too pushy.

"Yeah, that'd be cool," replied Pete, in his best James Dean.

As Billy left the kitchen to retrieve the plastic bag he had dropped off just inside the front door, he could hear the *mariachis* speaking in muted English. He was positive it was Juan from San Blas, who, once again, felt it necessary to inform his band-mates that he had never, ever heard of The Chicago Squires.

When Billy returned, he ceremoniously placed his bag of songs on the table for all to behold. He wasn't sure where to begin. Maybe the best thing to do he decided would be to start from scratch. Learn anew. Still, it would seem strange teaching "Hard Driven Rain" to three new musicians, in a different country, in another lifetime. *What the hell,* he thought, *let's see what happens.*

Withdrawing the appropriate pages from the bag, Billy distributed them around the table. "This is the song that made number three in the States. A guy named David Hanson and I wrote it, but we never thought it would become as big as it did. Maybe the best way for me to show you how it goes would be for me to start, and for you guys to jump in when you think you've got it. Okay?"

"Okay," replied John. "I will be honored to play so famous a song!"

Billy grinned.

The four adjourned to the living room "stage" and resumed their designated places.

Billy counted down and began to play. He played with passion. His guitar rang out on the cutting edge and his voice was strong and confident.

After a verse, Clint kicked in on the drums. The beat was simple, but strong — nothing fancy, just regular and hard. After the first chorus,

John had developed a bass line which was eerily similar to the one that David Hanson had thumped out in the original version of the top seller. By the second chorus, Pete had begun to experiment with a guitar lead, and was waiting for Billy to give him the go-ahead to cut loose. The signal was given. Pete's fingers flew.

The initial rendition of "Rain" ended with Clint's circling his drum kit, from snare to floor tom, with a pounding sequence of rolls. When he came down hard on the crash cymbal, the others matched him on bass and guitars. The final note resounded loud and true.

Silence ensued.

Billy was the first to break the spell. "Holy Christ!" Other expletives followed; some in Spanish, some in English.

By the end of the session, some four hours later, each young musician realized that magic had been created. No one attempted to verbalize what had occurred because no one could. Each knew intrinsically however, that he had participated in something very unique.

As Billy collected his songs, uttered the appropriate "see you laters," and began to depart, Pete asked the question which had been pressing upon everyone's thoughts throughout the entire afternoon: "What next, Billy?"

The others listened intently for the guitar slinger's response.

"I don't know. I never thought it'd be this good. I'll talk to you soon though. Promise.

Okay?"

"Okay," was all John could utter. "Sounds good."

An Ingenuous Reply

That night at work, when Assistant and Maria were both occupied with a large group of tourists from Mexico City, Hermano drew Billy aside, and in an intimate, almost collusive voice, asked, "How'd it go, my friend?"

Billy replied as honestly as he could. "I'm really not sure. I have to think."

A "Get Lost Trip" Kind of Day

It had been a restless night. Sleep had eluded the songwriter, and when it did come, it was sporadic.

At least, Rutherford had remained in his own bed.

Mixing his second obligatory cup of syrupy, black coffee, Billy decided today would be an ideal "get lost trip" kind of day. On days when there was nothing pressing to be accomplished or when he just wanted some time to himself, Billy would randomly board one of the town's rambling old buses, pay his fare and ride to the end of the line. Where the bus stopped, didn't much matter. When it did, he would depart and begin his explorations.

Once, Billy had discovered a pensive Rodan-like statue of John Huston in a plaza on Isla Rio Cuale. Below the celebrated director's likeness was a plaque stamped with his eulogy to Humphry Bogart.

On another occasion, Billy's stomach had churned for a week after he had eaten something from a styrofoam cup he had purchased at an open air fish market somewhere along Mismaloya Beach.

Today, Billy didn't care if he stumbled across anything new or not. All he wanted was a little time to think.

Climbing into the first ramshackle vehicle that stopped to pick up passengers, the young investigator rode until the rest of the travellers had thinned out along the way. Billy was now the sole rider. When the driver pulled over and signalled that the end of the route had arrived, Billy thanked him and stepped out onto the cobblestone street. Although the area was unfamiliar to him, he knew he had disembarked somewhere near the southern parameter of the city. Flipping a mental coin, Billy headed east.

After walking several blocks, he purchased a cold bottle of water and sat down in the shade of what appeared to be a small, children's playground. Billy's thoughts turned immediately to music. He enjoyed his occasional stints in the park, strumming on Hermano's old Martin, but it was nothing like playing good old-fashioned rock 'n' roll with some hot musicians — nothing like it at all. In fact, realized Billy, his new *mariachi* friends didn't even know how good they were. The ex-Squire had always thought of himself as a competent guitarist, but Pete had a knack for picking out tasteful leads Billy knew he could never rival. John's bass was rock solid in his hands. Clint was a metronome with drum sticks. All three, perhaps because of their need to blend voices as a trio, made harmonies appear effortless. They were quick studies as well. Billy realized his songs never sounded better than in their hands. Each musician would interpret Billy's lyrics and simple guitar chords in his own way and add subtle nuances to enhance the overall finished product. The end result somehow became greater than the sum of the individual parts.

Billy continued to let his thoughts ramble: *I don't even know these guys. I thought we all felt something good was happening, but I've been wrong before. I don't know. If we did get together, would Hermano feel pissed off or hurt? No, maybe not. He was the one who wanted me to go for it. If we did get a few gigs, maybe Maria could fill in for me. She's there all the time anyway.*

More musings: *I was right about Vallarta though. I took a chance. I had nothing to lose. I have a home. Songs are good. I feel good. Strong. Free. Some friends. Do it?*

His pondering was interrupted when a group of twenty or so squealing school children arrived with their teacher to reclaim their territory.

Billy rose from his bench and set off toward home.

By the time he arrived, he knew what he was going to do.

A Fine Sight and a Welcome Visitor

Business was exceptionally brisk in the park that evening. It was fortunate that Maria was again present. A cruise ship must have arrived earlier, judging by the number of plastic bracelets adorning the wrists of sun-deprived tourists who were eager to barter for anything made in Mexico. Assistant had little time to examine his worn out sandals. Hermano had plenty of time to smile, nod, and poke at his cheek. Billy made time to rehearse what he would say to his *mariachi* friends when he next encountered them.

The young man also stole a few minutes to glance secretively at the ever-enspirited Maria. His ogles seemed to coincide with the times she was either stretching up to withdraw something suspended from the sturdy twine strung across the awning or bending down to pick up an article from a cardboard box on the ground. *I hope Hermano is paying her well,* thought Billy in a big brotherly sort of way. *She sure is a hard worker.*

Man, she's got a great butt! This time, Billy thought of her as something akin to a fourteenth cousin.

"Hola, amigo!" Billy's lascivious thoughts were broken by Juan Flores' salutation.

"Oh... Hi, John! Sorry, I didn't even see you coming. I was...working."

"Yes," replied the man from San Blas with a straight face. "I can see that. How do you say?

149

Your job has some fringe benefits."

"Yep," answered Billy, "but I don't have any health coverage or a dental plan!"

Both laughed as John acknowledged Billy's co-workers with a wave of his hand.

The bassist continued: "Would you like to come by my house tomorrow and play some more? The other guys would really like it if you could."

"Sounds good, John. I'd really enjoy that."

"*Bueno*! And one more thing. We've been talking. Do you think you could bring some more of your songs? We would like to learn them."

"I can do that," answered Billy with pride. "I like it when the four of us play my stuff."

"Okay then! Come early! We'll crank up the amps and see what we can do!"

Billy paused before speaking. "Thanks, John."

John nodded and was off.

Billy and the Boys Come to Terms

An eager Billy Emmerson arrived at John's doorstep at twelve the next day. In his plastic bag, he carried copies of six songs the *mariachis* had never heard: three from the Squires' days and three written in Vallarta.

Once inside, after greetings and small talk had been exchanged, the four gathered in front of John's makeshift stage. Billy distributed his songs to each musician and jokingly added: "You think you guys can handle this stuff?"

"Just watch us, *hombre*!" exclaimed Pete.

"You start, Billy! We'll ride shotgun for awhile, then jump in." Clint was quick on the draw and confident in his aim.

Billy began. The others joined in. After a few hours, magic had been repeated. This time however, the four were even more cohesive. They seemed to anticipate each other's next move with ease and aplomb. When vocals needed to dominate, instruments were restrained and Billy was given free rein. If Pete let loose with a guitar solo, the other three would back him up and compliment his soaring notes. They played like clairvoyants.

At last, the amplifiers were silenced and the four adjourned to the kitchen for some cold libations and a much deserved break.

Billy was the first to plop down on a chair around John's small table. His white sleeveless T-shirt was drenched with sweat. His finger tips were red and tender. "Wow!" was the first word to fly from his dry throat.

"Wow!" repeated Pete.

"Shit!" exclaimed Clint.

John just grinned.

The musicians downed their Coronas in record time.

Billy felt the time had come to say something. *It's now or never!* he thought. The others seemed to read his mind. He had their undivided attention without speaking a word.

"Okay," began Billy, "what do you guys wanna do?" He thought the situation demanded he get straight to the point.

Clint answered for the rest. He was a straightshooter. "We want to make a group!"

"So do I," answered Billy.

The quartet shook hands.

A Forthcoming Fiesta of Much Magnitude

Reporting for his shift that night, Billy confronted his friend and employer before Hermano fled to the *farmacia* to court the vivacious Angelica. *"Compadre*, remember we talked about making some more music here soon?"

"Yes, Billy! It would be most festive. Maria could work and we could share our profits with her. Okay?" Hermano smiled and stabbed his cheek. "Business would be very, very good!"

"How 'bout next Saturday night?" Billy asked.

"Muy bueno! Good!" exclaimed Hermano. Peso signs were beginning to dance in his head.

"One more thing," added Billy. "Would it be okay if my friends played with me? We're sorta starting a band together."

"Okay?" asked the pudgy purser in mock disbelief. "It would be more than okay! I will make the posters and proclaim the event! It will be the fiesta of Hidalgo!"

Hermano suddenly grew silent. Grasping Billy's hand, he spoke in a whisper: "I am most happy, my friend."

"So am I, amigo," Billy answered. "So am I."

Billy's band-mates were more than amenable to performing in the park. When the American explained how he felt he owed Hermano a lot, all three understood the situation immediately and were quick to rally.

"*Vaqueros* who wear white hats should always stick together. Right, Billy?"

"Right, Clint," agreed Billy in a bad Gary Cooper inflection. "It's good to be back in the saddle again!"

Final Preparations

For Billy Emmerson, the next several days sped by faster than a fleet of Mexican taxis. His nights were spent hawking souvenirs and delving into the mysteries of the Spanish and English languages with Assistant. His days were filled with endless hours of refining his music with his new group.

Billy's band members, with some reluctance, agreed to revert back to their old acoustic instruments for the approaching event in the park. Hauling equipment wouldn't have been a problem, as Billy could have borrowed his employer's old pickup for the occasion, but he wasn't sure how the authorities would have reacted to high decibel rock 'n' roll without some sort of official permission. It would be easier this way. Pete, Clint, and John understood.

Hermano must have shed ten pounds in the last several days. He was a whirling dervish of dollars! He was the Tasmanian Devil of cartoon commerce!

Attached to every tree and lamp post in the park, was a small poster Hermano had designed and had reproduced announcing Saturday's gala affair. Some were printed in Spanish, others in English: "Billy Emmerson and his band! Parque Hidalgo! Saturday night! Big Fiesta! Gratuities much appreciated." When Billy purchased groceries, he spotted the signs in store windows. When he walked to John's for rehearsal, he saw them plastered on every palm tree on the Malecón. Twice, he noticed the announcements stuck to the rear windows of cars. No stone was left unturned.

Billy was beginning to appreciate Hermano's gift for turning a peso more and more.

Saturday night had come at last. When Billy arrived at the park, with his old Martin in hand, the walkways between the wrought-iron benches and the souvenir and food stands were already crowded with a diverse mixture of residents and tourists. The gargoyle street lamps, scattered throughout the grounds, seemed to glow with a festive warmth. Strands of mini-lights, draped below the awnings of each small establishment, reminded Billy of Christmas back home.

"Hola, amigo!" called Hermano with fervor and anticipation. "Are you prepared for the show?" The buttons on his shirt were fighting for freedom.

"I'm as ready as I'll ever be boss!" exclaimed Billy. "I just didn't expect this many people."

"Publicity, my friend! It's good for the business!" Hermano made a sweeping gesture of the park with his left hand while finding his cheek with his right.

That's gotta be hard to do, thought Billy.

"Also," continued Hermano, chest bulging even more, "I have set up three of the chairs which fold for the *mariachis*. The house of the fish has been placed in front of our shop so that I might personally supervise the matters of the

156

payment. It might be a good thought to leave the guitar case open and near you as well. I am expecting many peoples. Okay, Billy?"

"Okay!" Billy acquiesced, impressed with the vendor's attention to detail. "You've done a great job!"

Maria and Assistant were stationed behind the cart dealing with a couple, who seemed quite intent upon purchasing a large canvas bag imprinted with the words: "Made in Paradise!" When the transaction had been successfully completed, both young merchandisers emerged to greet Billy.

"Good luck tonight!" proclaimed Assistant. Maria smiled broadly.

"Thanks, partner," answered Billy. "It should be fun." Turning to the young woman, he added: "How are you tonight, Maria? You look very nice."

"Gracias, Billy," she replied demurely, yet with a mischievous glint in her eyes. "I know you will be very good."

"Thank you, amiga. I'm gonna try my best." *God, if her skirt were any tighter,* Billy thought, *she'd never be able to walk.*

"Hey, Billy!" Pete's exclamation abruptly dispelled the young musician's current train of thought.

Turning around, Billy responded with handshakes and salutations as Pete and his other band-mates clustered around. They seemed slightly apprehensive, as if waiting for some set of illuminating instructions. Billy tried to put his new friends at ease with smiles and verbal votes of reassurance. "You guys are gonna be great tonight! We know all the stuff and sound really good. There's nothing more we can do. Put your instruments down over here and we'll grab a beer before we start. Okay?"

"Okay," answered Clint. "My throat is as dry as a rattlesnake's belly in July!"

John and Pete smiled.

When the Modelo had been purchased, the four retreated behind the souvenir stand to sip their beer and make final preparations. Everyone was beginning to feel more relaxed. As the cans were drained, each musician realized that the band was ready.

"All set?" Billy asked.

"All set!" replied Pete, answering for the others.

As the quartet made their way to the makeshift stage, Billy was pleased to see familiar people scattered throughout the crowd. Although he couldn't attach names to some of the faces, he recognized them from his previous solo performances.

Assistant and Maria had assumed their positions behind the heavily laden shelves of the shop when the band had vacated. They were expecting a memorable evening.

Hermano and Angelica stood near the fish bowl smiling and holding hands.

Paco had arrived shortly after he had sold

beer to Billy and the band. Tonight, he was clutching a *sizable* brown paper bag.

As the four bandsmen seated themselves and checked the tuning of their instruments, Billy turned to Hermano, smiled, and nodded. Hermano repeated the gesture.

An Auspicious Debut

The performance proved more successful than Billy had hoped for. The songs seemed to have taken on a life of their own. All the musicians did was nurture them. Encores were bestowed graciously. Congratulations were dispensed freely.

By night's end, all Hermano could do was to stare in disbelief at the over-flowing fish bowl and guitar case. His finger seemed glued to his cheek.

Angelica giggled and jiggled.

Assistant shuffled.

Maria bounced with unspent energy.

Paco proved himself a happy drunk.

Billy couldn't remember hitting the bed that evening.

The Wanderers

Early Sunday morning, after feeding Rutherford and brewing his first cup of coffee, Billy had time to reel in some half-submerged ideas. Peering out onto the boulevard at the old tamarind tree, he allowed his thoughts to flow like the sun washing over the tree's twisted branches: *Sand. Blue Skies. Palm trees. Cold beer. Comfortable home. Needs were not great. Bills were paid. Time for exploring. Time for doing nothing. Music. Always the music.*

The first step would be to consult his new band members. Billy was certain his plan would meet with no opposition.

Arriving at John's home around one that afternoon, and being admitted by the bassist, a resolute Mr. Emmerson was pleased that Pete and Clint were also present. It would be more expedient if everyone received the proposal at once.

The *mariachis* usually rehearsed during the afternoons and set about on their rounds at sunset. Today was an exception. Rather than practicing their tight harmonies, the trio seemed intent on reliving the previous night's success. Billy readily joined in. The laughter that ensued was an outlet. No one was ready to come down from the plateau he had climbed.

During a brief lull in which John had gone to the kitchen to fetch beer, Pete decided to inform Billy of a discussion the three had held prior to the songwriter's arrival. Pete came directly to the point. "Look, Billy, before you came this afternoon we were talking about you and the band."

"Funny," Billy replied, "before I got here, I was thinking about the same thing."

John returned with the Coronas.

Billy continued. "Wanna hear what I think?"

"Go on, Billy. Shoot." Clint never ventured too far from his cowpoke persona.

"Okay. Here's my idea." Billy let the words fall where they may. "You guys have connections with a lot of the restaurants and hotels in town. What if you gave some names and addresses to Hermano? He's sharp and can talk his way into anything. He'd make a great manager. Haven't talked to him yet though. Wanted to see what you guys thought first. Hell, Assistant's smart too! Maybe he could be...well...an assistant. Maria could fill in for me whenever we're playing. Maybe we could play some nights and you guys could do your travelling minstrel thing other nights. What do you think? All I know is that I wanna play some rock 'n' roll!"

"Billy!" It was John's turn. "That's all we wanted to hear!"

Laughter and handshakes followed.

More ideas were verbalized.

"What'll we call ourselves?" Billy looked to his friends for input. "We can't call ourselves The Squires. That's already been tried."

"I don't know," replied Pete. "We never had a name. All we ever did was wander around and hope the tourists would like the music."

"Wait a minute!" exclaimed Billy. "That's it! The Wanderers! What do you think?"

"Billy and The Wanderers sounds better to me, amigo," added John.

Pete and Clint quickly concurred.

"Okay. Thanks, guys. Now we have a name." The young man from Chicago felt touched by his friends' gesture. "Wanna stop by the park tonight so we can talk to everybody?"

Proposals Solidified

Several hours later, in Hidalgo, details were discussed, questions asked, and thoughts bantered about freely.

In the end, Hermano had readily accepted the position of manager, Maria was pleased to fill in whenever it was required, and Assistant felt honored to be proclaimed..."assistant."

Billy and The Wanderers was on its way.

Another Ride on the Carousel

By November, 1984, Billy Emmerson and his band had played six major hotels and several prestigious restaurants throughout Vallarta. Each successive engagement had reaped more accolades than the previous.

This time around however, the leader of The Wanderers handled success differently. He knew it could be elusive and was determined not to make the same mistakes twice.

Rather than investing his earnings in the outward trappings of his newly elevated status, Billy chose to maintain the lifestyle he had come to appreciate. Gone were the days of fuzzy, half-lost memories and hangovers that never seemed to end. Glittering baubles, custom-made clothes, and underage groupies came last on Billy's list of priorities.

He still worked in the park, although less frequently as of late.

Hermano, Assistant, and Maria were all supportive of Billy's efforts and enjoyed their own measure of success as a result of being integral members of the team.

Angelica seemed to be gaining weight.

Under Billy's guidance and encouragement, the other members of The Wanderers had begun to explore their latent individual talents. Pete had purchased an electric keyboard and was becoming quite proficient at stringing together intricate chord conceptions. John's vocal harmonies were expanding at an exponential rate. Clint had decided to try his hand at writing. Most of his lyrics related to "good guys" verses "bad guys." The "good guys" always got the girl.

The band grew tighter.

The music grew stronger.

Each engagement attracted larger crowds than the performance before.

Hermano Proves Himself Quite an Impresario

On a scheduled night of souvenir duty, Billy
had barely taken the first step leading into the
park when he was confronted by his old
employer and new manager. The evening was
uncharacteristically cool and a fine rain was
beginning to collect in shallow puddles on the
cobblestone street. The rain did nothing
however to dampen Hermano's spirits.

"Billy, my boy! How are you? Good to see
you!" Hermano extended his beefy hand and
locked Billy's fingers in an inextricable grip.

"Whoa! I'm great, boss, but I need that hand
for playing!"

Both grinned and Hermano relinquished his
hold.

"Sorry, amigo, but I possess something
important I must discuss with you." Hermano
looked like he'd been caught with his hand in the
galleta jar.

"Sure. What is it, boss?" Billy was curious.

"Not here, Billy. Let's go across to La Scala
and sit down. There are hardly any peoples
tonight anyway, and our young friend and Maria
can look after the business."

Before the first round of beer arrived,
Hermano broached the subject of his most
pressing matter of inspiration.

"Listen to me, Billy and inform me of your
opinion. Christmas will be arriving in about six
weeks. You know that that is when *muchos*

167

many tourists arrive in Vallarta and spend their *muchos* many dollars. Right?"

"Right," agreed Billy. There was nothing to dispute.

"Did you also know that every year at Christmas, the Pacifico Grandé, the largest hotel in Vallarta, has a fiesta for which the tickets sell for one-hundred American dollars each?"

"No, I didn't know," replied Billy.

Hermano pressed on. "Did you know that hundreds of the peoples attend this glorious event?"

"Nope. You've got me again," conceded a slightly confused Billy.

"Then listen, amigo. What if I told you that you and your band would be assured of three-thousand, five-hundred American dollars if you played on the night of Christmas? What would you say if I told you that you could rehearse the music everyday on the stage and store the equipment at the hotel afterward?"

Billy was speechless. When he finally managed to regain most of his faculties, he reached across the table to shake his friend's hand. "I'd say you're one smart son-of-a-bitch!"

The beer tasted exceptionally good that night.

Back on Solid Wood

On the street, I'm just another man,
Someone who's just gettin' by,
But up on the stage, it's another world.
Got no gravity! I think I can fly.

-Fat Willy Washington, 1957

It didn't take Billy and The Wanderers long to adjust to the big stage. After about three days, the musicians had worked out any technical challenges the large hall had to present. With each practice, the performers grew less intimidated by their new surroundings and more confident that they could make their musical mark on the city by the beach.

Spectators, mostly guests of the hotel, began to appear at rehearsals. Since they remained quietly respectful when the band was diligently absorbed in refining new melodies, they were allowed to stay. Once a tune had been polished and deemed ready to perform, this ever-growing audience was employed as a sounding board for positive reinforcement by the band. The onlookers devoured the music and The Wanderers thrived on their approval.

A Stranger Arrives

After an afternoon when practice had progressed exceptionally well, Billy Emmerson decided to linger behind in order to complete a song he had begun a week ago. The rest of the group had packed up and set off for independent destinations. The bystanders had cleared the hall when rehearsal had ended. Slouching down on Clint's drum stool with head bent over his guitar, Billy strummed the old Martin in quest of a chord pattern which seemed to baffle him. Engrossed in his music, he never noticed as someone approached from the front of the stage.

"Hello?"

Slightly startled, Billy raised his head and acknowledged the voice. "Oh...uhh...Hello."

Standing with arms resting upon the elevated hardwood, was the most striking looking woman the young man had ever seen. Her short auburn hair framed a face which was delicate and sensual at the same time — coal-black eyes, pouting full lips, a small straight nose, and, skin the colour of honey. From her position in front of the stage, Billy could only guess her height to be somewhat over five-foot six. She appeared in her mid-twenties.

The stranger spoke next. "I heard you practicing this afternoon and I thought the band sounded great."

"Thanks. I don't know about that, but we have a lot of fun and the people seem to like the music," Billy replied, feeling more comfortable.

"They sure do! I came back knowing you were practicing by yourself. I hope I'm not bothering you, but I have to ask you about one of the songs."

"Sure. Go 'head."

"I heard you do 'Hard Driven Rain.' Is that the only song you do that's not original? I've got the single at home by The Chicago Squires and I think it's really good. Is that why you play the song? Is it because you think it's as good as I do?"

Billy arose from his stool with a smile on his face. "Come on up and I'll tell you about it." He motioned to a set of stairs to the left leading up to the stage.

As the young woman ascended the steps, Billy noticed that he had probably judged her height to be about right. He also noticed her long , muscular legs emerging from tight black denim shorts and her small, firm breasts covered only by a plain matching T-shirt.

When she had glided to within greeting distance, Billy extended his hand and introduced himself. "Hello, again. My name's Billy Emmerson."

"Hello, again to you," she replied, accepting his hand.

Billy thought she had a perfect smile.

"My name's Irena Quinn. Now that I know your name, I think I know why you do that Squires' tune so well."

"Wanna hear a story, Irena?" Billy prayed to the gods of rock 'n' roll that she would.

"I'd love to." Irena spoke in a near whisper without hesitation.

Reciprocities

Two hours later, stories had been exchanged. Billy had never talked so much in his life. With Ruby, there had been honesty, but it was somehow tinged with a sense of urgency coupled with fatalism. With Irena, time was somehow not a limiting constraint.

When a question arose, Billy answered with veracity. Irena responded with equal candor to his inquiries yet, somehow, Billy felt she was holding something back.

Irena Quinn had been born in New York City and had lived there her entire life. Her father was an importer from the city and had met her mother twenty-eight years ago while on a business trip to Mexico City. The two had fallen in love, settled in the States, and had begun a family two years later when Irena was born. Irena had begun working for her father immediately after college, but it was not until the past few years that the business had begun to flourish. Irena liked to think she was a contributing factor. Both parents thought a prolonged vacation was long overdue. Since Irena had never been to Mexico, the Quinns believed the time was opportune to help her discover a part of her heritage. After visiting with, and enjoying the company of several relatives in Mexico City, the family set off for the beaches of Vallarta. The Pacific beckoned. They were in no hurry to return to New York.

"Why did you wait so long before coming to Mexico?" inquired Billy.

"Why did you wait so long?" countered the señorita with a teasing smile.

"Okay, we're even." The one-time Chicogoan blushed slightly, but returned Irena's smile.

For Billy, it seemed a physical impossibility to gaze anywhere but at this mesmerizing lady from New York. For him, time stood still. He may have been rivetted to her for several seconds or several hours. He was oblivious to the workings of the world.

Irena broke the spell. "Are you practicing here tomorrow?"

"Pardon? Oh, right. Yes. Sure. We're trying to get in as many sessions as we can before Christmas."

"Would it be okay if I sat up close and watched? I really like your stuff."

"It'd be more than okay." Billy hoped he wasn't crossing over some don't-seem-too-eager kind of line.

He wasn't.

"Okay, that would be great! See you tomorrow."

"*Hasta mañana*, Irena."

As the young woman descended the steps and exited through a side door of the ballroom, Billy Emmerson envisioned fire-breathing serpents and beautiful maidens.

Floating Above the Park

Because Hermano had much bigger plans for his young protégée, Billy's full-time assistance at the park was no longer deemed a necessity. He still reported for work several times a week, but Maria had proven herself a most capable salesperson and The Wanderers' new manager was more than amenable to having his promising client take time off to write, rehearse or do whatever musicians did.

Tonight however, Billy didn't feel much like working on songs. His mind was elsewhere. Besides, hawking ceramic necklaces required much less thinking.

"Hola, amigo!" called Hermano as Billy approached the cart on wheels. "Are you working at the business tonight? Many peoples are here!"

"Sure am, boss! Always glad to do my share. Besides, I thought you might like a little time with Angelica. How's she doing anyway?"

Hermano glanced toward the stars and sighed. "It is difficult to believe, my friend, but she is becoming more beautiful each time we encounter. She is always so happy! So full of girth!"

Billy suppressed a smile. "I think the word in English you seek is 'mirth,' amigo, but that's okay. I always know what you mean."

Work passed quickly that night.

Hermano took Billy's advice and stole off to court his voracious saraph.

Maria and Assistant sold their weight in souvenirs.

Billy smiled a lot.

A Beautiful Observer

"Billy, you're hot today, man! I've never heard you play like this!"

"Thanks, Pete. I guess I just feel really good today."

During the afternoon's practice, Billy could not keep his eyes from targeting Irena who was sitting alone at a table near the stage. When she met his looks with her own unfaltering gaze, the singer and rhythm guitarist discovered notes he never knew existed. The audience was entranced by the performance.

When rehearsal ended, and the spectators had dispersed after demonstrating their appreciation with steady applause, Clint turned to Billy and asked: "*Hombre,* you wanna pack up and head to the nearest saloon to wash the dust down?"

"No. Thanks anyway, pardner. You guys go ahead. There's someone I'd like to talk to."

Since Irena was the only one left in the hall, The Wanderers had no trouble in interpreting their leader's words or unspoken intentions. Instruments were quickly stashed and the *mariachis* left the stage singing something in Spanish. Something very lively.

Billy felt elated yet jittery at the same time. His mouth was dry, a thousand butterflies churned in his stomach, and he was positive that he would stumble as he left the stage.

He didn't trip. As he approached Irena's table, his smile grew wider. "Hi, Irena. Glad you could come today."

"Hi, Billy. You sounded fantastic! I didn't think you'd mind if I stuck around. Want to sit?"

Billy sat. He didn't fall over a chair. "I was really glad to see you today and I'm really glad you stuck around. Wanna do something?" Billy felt his color rise. He didn't want to scare this girl away. He had only known her for a day. "I'm sorry," he added at once. "I didn't mean to come out and seem so, ahh, forward, but when I saw you out there today, and you kinda looked back, I just thought you might, ahh..."

Irena smiled reassuringly, and quickly replied in an effort to assuage the young musician: "Billy, can I be honest with you?"

"Sure," he responded in a hushed voice. He was expecting the worst.

"I'd love to do something!"

Irena's open response and flashing smile prompted Billy to think of dragons once again. "That'd be great!" he exclaimed with relief.

"Why don't you give me an hour to change and do a couple of errands and we could go for a walk or something?" prompted Irena.

"You look good already, but that would be fine. It'll give me time to run home and shower. Rock 'n' roll is a sweaty business you know!" At this point, Billy was sure that his mouth was gaining the upper hand on his brain but, he really didn't care. This beautiful girl seemed so open with him that he seemed comfortable just being himself with her.

"Would you like to meet me here, Billy or come to our suite?" Irena didn't want Billy to feel uncomfortable, so a choice was offered. "My parents are nice."

Billy thought for a moment. His eyes were once again locked upon the resplendent face of the woman seated next to him. He replied quietly, but with conviction: "I think I'd like to meet your parents."

It was Irena's turn to hesitate. "Yes," she whispered, without losing eye contact, "I think that would be best."

After a definite time was arranged, and Irena had informed Billy of her room number, the two rose, almost reluctantly, as if they were afraid to shatter the moment.

"Okay?" Billy inquired.

"Okay," Irena assured him.

"See you in a bit."

"See you in a bit, Billy."

The Source of Progeny

Billy arrived at Irena's door at precisely seven o'clock. He knocked three times and waited. He was nervous. His palms were clammy. He felt he needed to shower again. Within seconds, the door swung open and Billy was greeted by the young lady who seemed to rob him of his senses every time he looked at her.

"Come on in, Billy. I told my parents you were coming. They'd like to meet you." Dressed casually in sandals, jeans, and a sleeveless white top, Irena exuded a radiance which seemed to blind her weak-kneed suitor.

"Well...umm...thank you."

Stepping into the large foyer, Billy was met by a tall, husky gentleman who, Billy presumed, must be Irena's father. Mr. Quinn appeared in his mid-fifties, an inch or so taller than Billy, heavier, ruddy complexioned and with reddish hair beginning to gray. He smiled, extended his burly hand, and greeted Billy with open warmth. "Nice to meet you, young man. Irena has told me you're a mighty fine singer. I love to sing myself, especially after a few pints!"

"Nice to meet you, Mr. Quinn," replied Billy as he shook the big man's hand.

"My name's Mike, son. Mr. Quinn's my father's name!"

Billy grinned. He was beginning to feel more at ease.

"Come on, Billy. I'd like you to meet my wife."

Following Mr. Quinn into the living room, Billy soon found himself standing directly in front of a lady seated demurely on a plush davenport below a large picture window. Mrs. Quinn portrayed the image of sublimity and elegance. Her features were as fine as Irena's, but her complexion much darker. Long, black lashes framed eyes the color of sepia. Thick, ebony hair was held back in a single braid. She was attired in a traditional, white embroidered dress which seemed to wrap itself delicately over her slim figure.

" *Buenas noches, señora .*"

For a moment, as Billy lightly grasped her slender hand, he felt a look pass between them which seemed to draw him into some unknown conspiratorial bond. She smiled and the feeling passed.

"Would you like to sit down and have something cold to drink, Billy?"

Before Billy could reply, Irena's father made the decision for him. "Oh, let the young folks go, Katie! They don't want to hang around some old fogies when they could be out enjoying themselves on the town. Besides, I was thinking of a drink or two myself and being alone with you!"

Mrs. Quinn laughed and spoke to Billy in Spanish. She told him that her big Irish husband was a good man, but just a little *loco.*

Irena crossed the room and took Billy by the hand. "Okay, we'll see you later then. We won't be late." She was glowing with pride at the open affection her parents displayed with one another and at the effort they had made in making Billy feel comfortable. Irena relinquished her hold on her young courter and spontaneously hugged each of them.

When embraces ended, Irena reclaimed Billy's hand and the couple initiated their departure. Billy expressed his pleasure at having met Mr. and Mrs. Quinn and his hopes that he might see them again.

Mrs. Quinn, with her arm encircling her husband's waist, looked directly at her daughter's caller and spoke: "It was good meeting you, Billy. I hope we'll see you soon. I know we will." She smiled. Billy was again drawn into the realm of veiled confidence.

Once outside the closed door, Irena turned to Billy and asked teasingly: "There, that wasn't so bad was it?"

"Nope, not bad," he replied. "Not bad at all."

Twinkle Lights Abound Overhead
(Not Those Strung Across Awnings)

After a few moments walk from the hotel, the couple found themselves strolling leisurely along the Malecón in a southerly direction toward Los Arcos. Although few words had been exchanged, both found themselves smiling incessantly.

Finally, Billy spoke. "Irena, this is really strange to me. I wanted to see you, but I don't have a clue where to go or what you'd like to do. I feel like a lost puppy. I'm just trying to be honest with you. I've been grinning like a fool, but I don't want you to think I'm one. I feel really weird. I..."

Irena took his hand. "Billy, you don't have to be anything you're not. Not with me. Why do you think I've been so quiet? I'm not sure what you want me to say. I think maybe that...I really don't know what I'm saying!"

Billy laughed. He took Irena's other hand in his. "Okay, look," he said, "I'm not sure what's happening here, but I know it's something good. I'm a little scared and I think you are too, but I'm not afraid to take a chance and see where it leads. Life's too short. How 'bout you? Will you take a chance, Irena?"

"Yes, Billy. I'll take a chance. Maybe I don't have the right, but I want to. I really want to."

The night was spent walking and talking. There was no pre-set destination. The conversation took them where it would. Irena spoke, Billy listened; Billy spoke, Irena listened. Both spent a lot of time stopping to look at each other. By the end of the evening, they both knew that something special had occurred.

When the two finally arrived at Irena's door, Billy took Irena's hands in his and looked down into the face of the beautiful sorceress who had enchanted him so completely. "Will you be at rehearsal tomorrow, Irena?"

"Yes."

"Can I see you after?"

"You don't have to ask."

"Irena, what happened tonight?"

"I don't know, Billy."

"You know the strange part?"

"Yes, I do. I don't think it's going to go away."

"Do you want it to?"

"Maybe it's not fair to you, Billy." Irena's eyes began to moisten, but her gaze remained unbroken.

"That's not what I asked. I asked if you wanted this to end. You said you'd take a chance. I don't care about fair or anything else. I care about you."

"And I care about you — maybe too much, but no, I don't want it to end."

Billy smiled.

Irena smiled back and squeezed his hands tighter. Tears were beginning to trickle down her face.

"You okay?"

"I'm okay. These are happy tears."

That night, Billy fell asleep somewhere in Camelot. The dragons were benevolent.

Irena Wins Over The Wanderers

At a little after noon, Billy and the rest of the band were beginning to set up for the day's session.

The songs were getting tighter and the musicians' confidence was increasing with every note they played.

As Irena entered the hall and seated herself at a small table near the stage, Billy immediately ceased his endeavors to fine tune his guitar and descended the stairs to meet her before the rest of The Wanderers knew he was missing.

"Hi, Irena. Glad you could make it."

"Did you think for a second that I wouldn't?" Irena did her best to feign hurt, but a quick smile soon put an end to her teasing.

"Well, anyway," replied Billy, countering with his own banter, "I'm glad you got here before the rest of the beautiful girls did. I wouldn't know which one to serenade!"

Both laughed.

"Irena?"

"Yes, Billy?"

"I missed you."

"Billy?"

"Yes?"

"I missed you too."

This time, they only smiled. Seconds passed interminably.

"Well...I guess I'd better get back to work. The guys are probably thinking I've abandoned them for somebody better looking." Billy knew it would be a great practice. When he reluctantly tore his eyes from the mystifying Miss Quinn, and glanced back up at the stage, he could see his band-mates seated on the edge of the hardwood platform staring down at him and Irena. All three were smiling and giving him the "thumbs up" gesture.

Billy turned to his companion. "My friends're a little off the wall, but they're really good guys. Would you like to meet them?"

"I sure would," Irena answered while rising. "I'm sure they can't be as crazy as we are though." She was still smiling.

"No way!" Billy exclaimed. With exaggerated sincerity, he added: "I don't feel the same about *them* as I do about you either."

Both joined hands and climbed the steps to the stage.

They were greeted by The Wanderers, who, by this time, had formed a straight, regimented line in front of their lead singer's microphone. They looked eager to meet the exotic looking stranger. They looked eager to pass muster.

Billy made the introductions. "Irena, this is John, our bass player. He is also known as 'Juan from San Blas.' John's the best. John, this is Irena."

"Nice to meet you, John." Irena smiled and offered her hand.

"Good to meet you too, Irena." John shook hands and smiled back.

"Next," continued Billy, "we have Pete. Pete's a great guitar player and is also getting pretty good on keyboards."

"Hi, Pete."

"Hi, Irena."

Again, Irena extended her hand and the two shook.

"Finally," resumed Billy, "I'd like you to meet Clint, Irena. Clint's our drummer and is one of the finest I've ever worked with."

While the previous introductions had been simple and brief, Clint was not one to settle for brevity when in the presence of such a captivating woman. "How do you do, miss?" He accepted Irena's hand and pumped it vigorously. Clint persisted: "You know, I've been from one end of this great country to the other, and, if you don't mind me saying so, you're prettier than a new-born calf in May! Once, in Tampico, I saw a piano player with hair the color of a Jersey cow in the sunshine. I thought she was a right handsome woman, but you're even easier to look at than she was! She could sing though. Sounded just like a young Gene Autry. Billy is lucky to have roped a good lookin' heifer like you!"

Irena smiled demurely and interjected in the hope of ending Clint's well-meaning string of compliments and bovine imagery: "Thank you, Clint for the kind words. You certainly know how to turn a girl's head!"

Clint seemed pleased that his efforts at

gallantry had been appreciated.

Taking Irena's hand in his, Billy regained her attention and exclaimed proudly to her: "Well, now that you've met everyone, let me walk you back to the table so you won't be such a distraction to these guys. We still have a lot of work to do before Christmas."

"You sound great already," replied Irena, "but if you really have to get to work, I'll leave you alone. I can find my way back to the table. And one more thing though..." Irena stretched up and whispered in Billy's ear: "Am I a distraction to you?"

Billy looked down at her and whispered back: "You sure are, but you're the best distraction I've ever had in my life." Reluctantly, he watched Irena descend the stairs and resume her seat at the table.

The room was beginning to fill with regular patrons. Instruments had been finely honed. Arrangements had been scrutinized meticulously.

It was Clint who unleashed the music. Striking his drum sticks together while barking into his microphone in syncopation, he liberated the first song. "Two, three, four!" "Bandaras Bay Blues" rocked.

After a gruelling three hours, The Wanderers felt confident the practice had been a success. The audience agreed and expressed vociferous support of the group's efforts.

When the instruments had been properly stored and locked away, Billy hurriedly bid *hasta mañana* to his friends and rushed to join Irena at her table.

"How do you think it went?" he asked, still breathless from the session.

"It was the best!" proclaimed Irena. "You're going to blow everyone away at Christmas!"

"Thank you," answered Billy. "It means a lot to me what you think. Are you going to be here with me at Christmas?"

"I really want to be, Billy. There's nothing in the world that I'd like more."

For a brief moment, Billy thought that he had detected something in Irena's eyes that had expressed a cloud of undesired doubt. The look soon dissipated however, and was quickly replaced by a smile that made Mr. Emmerson wonder upon which planet he resided.

"I have to go home and get cleaned up," he stammered, once he landed back in reality. "I have to feed Rutherford too. You remember the roommate I told you about. Check out my cactus plants. Cacti or cactuses are both. accepted plurals, you know. Maybe they need water. Maybe later, I could call on you or something. We could get something to eat if you like. Then, maybe we could go to Hidalgo and I could introduce you to my boss and friends I told you about. If you're not busy, I mean..."

Irena giggled and asked directly: "Billy Emmerson, formerly of The Chicago Squires, presently employed as a member of Billy and The Wanderers, are you asking me out on a date?"

"I guess I am."
"Well then, I guess I accept."

A Portentous Sensibility

A short time later, Billy found himself knocking on Irena's door. He had enjoyed meeting the Quinns and had no trepidations about encountering them again. Each time he saw Irena however, he felt like he was coming down with some unknown malady. Billy didn't dislike the feeling, but it was just such an unfamiliar experience that he didn't know what to make of it. He was sure however, that the poets were wrong. His heart seemed to beat regularly. It was his stomach that seemed to be acting up.

Mr. Quinn opened the door. "Hello, Billy! How are you doing? Come on in. Irena! Billy's here!"

"Thanks, Mr. Quinn. I'm fine. How about you, sir?" Billy entered.

"I'm great, my boy! Name's Mike though. I think the sun agrees with me. Look at my tan! I'm darker than Irena!"

Billy looked, but Mr. Quinn still appeared to emit a reddish glow.

From somewhere behind Mr. Quinn's formidable shadow, Irena's mother emerged, took Billy's hand, and stated with a wink: "If Mike gets any darker, people will start to think he's Mexican!"

"Well, you both look good," replied Billy diplomatically. "This Mexican sun brings out the best in people."

"I'm sure you're right," answered Mrs. Quinn.

Irena now joined the group from what Billy assumed was her adjoining bedroom.

"Hi, Billy."

"Hi, Irena." Billy's stomach was beginning to knot.

"I hear you two are going out for dinner tonight," interjected Mr. Quinn. He felt he should say something to break the silence as his daughter and her caller continued to gaze at each other in aphony.

Irena was jostled back to the present by her father's statement. "Oh, right, Dad. We are. Then we might walk over to Hidalgo later. Billy has some friends he'd like me to meet."

"Sounds good!" continued Mr. Quinn. "You two have a great time."

Irena and her parents hugged briefly.

The Quinns warmly expressed their pleasure at seeing Billy again.

As the two young people set out for the evening, Mrs. Quinn focussed exclusively on Billy and reiterated whimsically: " I hope you're right about the sun."

Surf 'n' Turf

Irena thoroughly enjoyed the food at La Scala, and was delighted when her escort joined in on an impromptu chorus of "La Bamba" rendered in high spirits by a three piece travelling band meandering its way through the restaurant in quest of spare pesos.

At around six-thirty, Billy could see the lights beginning to come to life across the street in Hidalgo. The few wrought-iron bars defining the open window at La Scala did little to obstruct his view. He was beginning to grow restless. He wanted to show off his beautiful companion to his friends. He wanted Irena to understand how the colors and scents of the park had enthralled him so many months ago. He wanted her to witness gargoyles guarding their eggs atop ancient street lamps. He wanted her to taste the food, watch the people, and listen to the sounds. He wanted to buy her a gaudy T-shirt. Most of all, Billy wanted Irena to understand why this was his home.

"What do you say, Irena? Are you up to meeting some more of my friends?"

"Sure. Sounds good. I just hope that Hermano is around. You told me his courting is in full swing." Irena added: "I'd like to meet Angelica too."

"Oh, I'm sure you will," answered Billy. "I'll bet you hit it off really well. By the way, do you like crêpes?"

Leaving the restaurant, crossing the cobblestones hand-in-hand, and climbing the few steps leading to the park, the couple treaded toward Hermano's portable business. Billy was pleased to observe that all of his amigos seemed busily engaged in preparing for the evening's festivities.

Hermano was the first to notice their approach and had deserted his post to greet them. "Hello, my friend! How are you doing?" Although Hermano was addressing Billy, his eyes seemed glued upon Irena.

Billy took the lead. "Irena, this is my boss, manager, and friend, Hermano. Hermano, *mi amiga*, Irena."

"I am very pleased to meet the acquaintance, señorita," replied Hermano with great eloquence.

"I am very happy to meet you as well, señor. Billy has told me many wonderful things about you."

Hermano blushed slightly as the two shook hands. He resumed: "I believe, señorita that the poets and the *músicos* like to make the little stories grow into the tall stories."

The two laughed, and Irena, feeling more comfortable, initiated a conversation in Spanish with the personable entrepreneur. Although Billy was not able to fathom the complete dialogue, he was almost certain the excerpts concerning him were quite complimentary.

When the talk appeared to wind down, Billy was pleased to see Hermano extend his arm to

Irena and begin a course of steps that would soon lead them to the front of the souvenir stand. Assistant and Maria had been busily pretending to arrange knick-knacks on the shelves since the arrival of the couple, but were far more interested in Billy's friend than in coffee mugs and paper weights. When looks could be stolen, they were. When heads needed to be cocked to catch elusive bits of conversation, they were bent discretely.

As Hermano and Irena drew near, the young employees suspended their charade and stood anxiously awaiting introductions. Spanish was the language of preference and, again, the conversation was animated and punctuated with laughter. Since Billy had been abandoned several paces behind, he had no idea of the content of the discussion.

Several moments passed and Billy was almost relieved to see Irena return to his waiting station alone.

His friends remained in front of the cart grinning as if they were privy to some intimate disclosure.

"What did you guys talk about?" asked Billy. "Was it good? Did you say anything about me?"

"We talked a little about you," Irena admitted. "Mostly though, we spoke about writers and musicians in general."

"What about them?"

"Well," answered Irena, "we came to the consensus that they were all a bit eccentric and even egotistical when it came to their work."

"But, look at me, Irena," asserted Billy. "I'm not like that at all."

"Of course you're not," she purred. "You're definitely an exception to the rule."

Billy smiled and thought to himself: *This girl's not only gorgeous, she's bright too.*

"Would you like to take a walk around the park, Irena? Maybe later we could see what's happening on the Malecón."

"That sounds beautiful. I can't believe how it's starting to fill up! I'd love to walk around and just soak everything in. I'd love to walk anywhere with you."

Billy sparkled.

The two strolled leisurely through Hidalgo for the better part of an hour. They sampled crêpes on a park bench while the scents of frying onions and sweet peppers wafted through the night air. They observed travelling merchants selling everything from brightly colored helium-filled balloons to pink and blue cotton candy in transparent plastic bags. They examined trinkets and toys at every booth. At Bruno's stand, Billy purchased a small wooden cross suspended on a black string necklace in which Irena had expressed a definite interest. Irena hugged Billy in appreciation of the gift. Bruno seemed delighted in his friend's happiness and good fortune.

When it seemed the pair had explored every square foot of the park, they crossed the cobblestones and set off to investigate the treasures of the Malecón.

They were not disappointed in their finds. By moonlight, the couple watched dolphins frolicking in the bay and fishing boats setting out for one last catch. They breathed in the salt air and listened to gentle waves lap the shore of the Pacific. Billy had experienced it all before, but tonight everything seemed new to him.

Too soon, the evening ended and Billy found himself standing at Irena's door once again searching her black eyes for the secret that had eluded him his entire life.

"Thank you for a wonderful night, Billy. I really enjoyed myself," Irena whispered. "My necklace is beautiful. I love it."

"I'm glad you had a good time. I really did," responded Billy in muted tones of his own.

The lady stood silent.

"Look," Billy continued, "I'm really not sure where to go from here."

After a slight pause, Irena offered a solution. "Maybe, you should say and do what your heart tells you. Maybe, you should keep taking those chances you told me about."

"Maybe, you're right."

Billy kissed her for the first time. The kiss was tender at first, then built to a swelling crescendo. When it ended, both pulled away unwillingly from each other's arms. Billy Emmerson had found his elusive secret. Excalibur was his.

The young musician spoke first. "Irena, I love you."

The young woman answered. "Billy, I love you."

"Irena's Song": Composed the Next Morning

In another world,
In another time,
Our souls were joined as one,
And our love was so strong,
That it wouldn't die,
When our time on Earth was done.
And through the years,
We drifted,
Never feeling the sun or the rain,
Until we touched,
And laughed and cried,
And found ourselves again.
For now I know when I hold you,
And memorize your face,
I'll find you again,
In another world,
In another time and place.

-William Emmerson, 1984

Courtship

For the next two weeks, Billy and Irena were inseparable.

Each day, Irena would listen to her enamored guitar player practice with The Wanderers and, each day, she came to appreciate, more and more, just how good the band was. The sheer volume of the fans jamming the practice hall seemed to increase on a daily basis, but Billy sang only to Irena. He had not yet performed "Irena's Song" for her or shown it to the rest of the group. He had special plans for his latest composition.

Once rehearsal had finished for the day, the couple would often beach comb, visit the shops on the island dividing the Rio Cuale or, simply venture forth on "get lost trips."

During late afternoons, they would frequently dine with the Quinns. Billy had grown increasingly fond of Irena's parents and had developed an easy rapport with them built on admiration and respect. The Quinns' feelings toward their daughter's open admirer were reciprocal. Laughter and good conversation always abounded at the dinner table.

Occasionally, Irena and Billy would climb the cobblestones to Billy's apartment and do their own cooking. Cheeseburgers were still the primier choice of cuisine for the ex-Chicagoan and Irena prepared them just right. Even Rutherford seemed to look forward to Miss Quinn's visits. He particularly appeared to enjoy the way she hand-fed him small, carefully torn bits of lettuce from her own plate.

When the sun had begun to set, leisurely walks along the Malecón or aimless hiking throughout the back streets of Vallarta had developed into the two's favorite evening activities. The couple never ceased to be amazed at the sights and prizes they would unexpectedly discover while rambling the city.

Since Billy's services at the souvenir shop had been reduced to occasional token appearances, he and Irena had been given ample opportunities to join Hermano and Angelica for numerous dinners at La Scala and other restaurants scattered throughout the city. Dinners would often be followed by crêpe sampling in the park. Crêpe sampling in the park frequently led to ice-cream sampling along the Malecón. Billy and Irena always enjoyed themselves on these occasions but made sure they endeavored to do more than their customary share of walking the next day. Somehow, Billy was not convinced that Angelica and his boss were *quite* as conscientious.

An Unexpected Revelation

On an early Saturday morning, a week before Christmas, Billy Emmerson and Irena Quinn had climbed steadily for about two hours from Billy's apartment on Hallowe'en Street, in an easterly direction, up into the jungle. Iguana spotting was their goal. The sightings were numerous, but the day had grown uncomfortably warm and humid. Both explorers were drenched in sweat, and each was more than ready to head back toward town for something cold to drink. Water bottles had been drained an hour ago.

"Billy, do you mind if we sit down for a minute before we start back?"

"Not at all. I've just about had it too. I hope those crêpes aren't catching up with us." Billy smiled.

Irena didn't reply. She found a shady resting place on a fallen tree along the main path, sat, buried her face in her hands, and, began to sob.

Immediately rushing to her side, Billy was too shaken to know how to respond. Kneeling before her, he gently placed both of his hands on her knees and asked in a quivering voice: "Irena, what's wrong? Please tell me. I love you."

Upon hearing these words, Irena flung her arms around Billy's neck and pressed her face next to his. "Oh, Billy, I love you so much." Tears flowed from her black eyes.

Billy hugged her tightly. "Tell me, please."

Tears from his blue eyes intermingled with hers. "Please," he whispered.

Slowly pulling her face from Billy's, until she met his pleading eyes, Irena spoke slowly and softly: "I've never lied to you, Billy. I love you with all my heart, but there are things I didn't tell you."

Neither made any attempt to hold back emotions.

"Tell me now, Irena! Nothing can change how I feel. I'll always love you!" Billy wept openly.

"I'll always love you too, Billy, but sometimes bad things happen. I'm frightened, Billy, really scared!" Irena's entire body shook.

The two clung together as if they would drown without each other's support.

After a moment, Irena spoke. "Just listen, okay, Billy? Don't talk."

Billy nodded.

"This trip has been the best thing that's ever happened to me. My mum and dad love it here too, maybe as much as I do, but it's not the only reason we came.

"I have a disease, Billy. It's a cancer. In the States, I was terribly sick. I went through everything — chemo, bone marrow transplants, experimental treatments, everything they threw at me. I went into remission. I was doing fine for awhile, then things started to go bad again.

"We came to this country to try different things — alternatives. They seem to be working. I feel fine, just a little tired sometimes.

"In a couple of days, we're flying to Mexico City for some tests. Everything's going to be fine, but there's always a chance..."

Billy could no longer remain silent. "What are you saying? Do you mean...you could still be sick? You could..."

"It could happen."

"No! It can't happen! Not now! Why?" A gamut of emotions churned inside Billy's body at the same time. Like acid, it was burning him alive.

"I don't know why, Billy. I only know it is happening. I know something else too. I know I'll love you no matter what."

Neither could speak. It wasn't necessary. In a trance, they found their way back to town and to Irena's suite.

"You alright, Billy?"

"I'm okay. It'll be fine. I'll...talk to you tomorrow."

"Do you want to come in?"

"No. I..."

"Billy?"

"Yes."

"I need you."

"I need you too, Irena. Without you...I..."

"It's okay, Billy."

They embraced for an eternity. Tears were beginning to well in their eyes once again.

Billy Emmerson knew he must leave now. He touched Irena's face and departed.

The Demons Rage

For the rest of the afternoon, and into the early evening, Billy needed to be alone. He locked himself away in his apartment. He drank tequila. He cursed God, His Son, and the Mother of Jesus. He cried. He drank more tequila. He cursed the world. At around eight, he passed out, not caring if he ever awoke.

Sunday

Billy did awaken. He awoke to the ringing of church bells.

The leader of The Wanderers phoned John and cancelled the afternoon's practice. The situation was explained briefly. John assured Billy that everyone would understand. The band was ready. There were more important matters to which Billy should attend. Billy thanked his bass player and promised to talk to him soon.

A short time later, the emotionally drained young man stood staring blankly at the Quinns' door. He didn't know what to say or how to act. He only knew that he must be with the girl hidden within. Billy knocked. The door was opened by Mr. Quinn.

"Come on in, son. We've been expecting you."

Billy was unable to speak. He nodded at Irena's father and entered. Mrs. Quinn and Irena arose from the davenport across the room holding hands. They had been crying. All four met somewhere in the middle of the room. All four embraced silently.

Billy was the first to break down.

Throughout the remainder of the day, Billy and the Quinns talked. They talked about life, and death, and, most of all, love. There were intervals when tears could not be contained but, moments of laughter as well.

It was well into the evening when Billy

decided to leave the family in order to give them time to be alone. He arose from the kitchen table around which everyone had been sitting and began his farewells.

It was Irena's mother who cut his attempts short. "We don't want you to leave tonight, Billy. Our daughter needs you here."

Billy and King Arthur's sword sat up all night on the couch guarding the kingdom from all things evil.

Irena's Departure

While Mr. and Mrs. Quinn pretended to get some last minute packing done before the short trip to Mexico City that morning, Billy and Irena were left together to finalize some details of their own. The two sat together near the window holding hands and speaking in whispers that were often broken when emotions overpowered words.

"You know I can't go to the airport with you, Irena."

"I know, Billy."

"Do you know why?"

"Yes. I do."

"Will you be back for Christmas?"

"Of course I will. I'll be in the front row watching."

"I'll be waiting for you, Irena. Wear the necklace I bought you, okay? It'll bring good luck."

Irena touched her wooden cross and promised Billy that she would wear it forever.

"Then we have a date for Christmas. I'll get going now, but I'll see you in a few days." Billy's voice was quaking, but he tried to conceal his fears with a thin smile.

"We've got a date, Mr. Emmerson."

Both rose and Irena walked Billy to the door.

"Say good-bye to your parents for me. I can't seem to..."

"It's okay. I will."

"Irena?"

"Yes, my heart."

"I will never love anyone but you. I can't. Don't ever..."

"I know. You don't have to say a word. Everything will be fine. You can't get rid of me so easily. I'm here forever. It's just a few days. Then we can..."

Billy threw his arms around her and held her like he wanted to melt into her every pore. He broke away and left quickly. He had to.

The Final Week

Billy explained what had happened to his friends in Hidalgo. He appreciated their embraces and words of understanding.

Billy followed routine. He needed routine.

Practices went well, although their were times when Billy's guitar suddenly needed tuning halfway through a melody, even though no false notes were detected. The Wanderers understood.

Billy fed Rutherford.

He watered his cacti.

He scrutinized the old tamarind tree on the boulevard.

The young man cried himself to sleep at night. He needed Irena. His heart was aching.

Now or Never

By eight-thirty Christmas evening, the hall of the Pacifico was crowded with onlookers waiting to witness the debut of the band which was causing such a huge stir throughout the city.

The stage was set. Instruments were tuned. Amplifiers were set to standby. The Wanderers knew this was their big chance. They were ready.

Billy had phoned Irena seven times over the last two days. He had knocked upon her door another five times. No response. What could have happened? Where was she?

By eight fifty-five, the band had assembled on stage. Billy could see the faces of his friends in the crowd. They had been through a lot together. He didn't want to let them down. He scanned the expressions of his band-mates, trying to read their thoughts. They were counting on him.

At precisely nine o'clock, Billy Emmerson strapped on his guitar and gestured to The Wanderers to meet him in front of Clint's drum kit. In hushed tones, so that his words would not be picked up by Clint's microphone, he spoke evenly and directly: "I'm okay. You guys wanna kick some ass?"

Billy could tell by their broad grins that they were more than willing to affirm to his question.

Each musician assumed his designated position. Stepping up to his mic at center stage, Billy swept the crowd with his eyes, paused briefly, and announced: "Ladies and gentlemen, thank you for coming tonight! We are Billy and The Wanderers!" He looked back at Clint and nodded. Clint banged out the time with his sticks. The band broke into its first number.

About five minutes later, Clint broke a drum stick on his crash cymbal as the last chord of "Don't Eat the Worm!" bounced off the walls. Each musician stared blankly ahead and held his breath. Then came the applause. It was shattering. It was intense. It was uproarious. There was a standing ovation punctuated with whistles and shouts. Each of The Wanderers exhaled. They had done it!

Billy was elated. He wanted the moment to last forever. Never had he experienced a feeling like this! At the same time, however, he wondered if he could maintain his resolve for another three hours. His heart was elsewhere, but he realized he was not the center of the universe. Irena was. He would somehow dig down and find the hidden resources to make her proud.

The next three sets brought the house down. The musicians couldn't complete a break without the audience screaming for them to reappear from off-stage. It was a rock 'n' roll fantasy come true.

Throughout every minute of every song, Billy constantly peered through the bright spotlights, down the center aisle, hoping against hope that Irena would appear. She never did.

As mid-night approached, Billy was thankful

there was only one more song to perform. He was drained. He had played the last two or three tunes mechanically. His talent and skill had kicked in as his emotions had begun to override the music.

The audience hadn't noticed.

Once again, summoning The Wanderers together before their final number, the exhausted songwriter tried desperately to inspire confidence and maintain exhilaration. "Okay, guys, one more song! One more, that's it! Let's make it our best! Let's show 'em..." Billy's voice trailed off to a place far away. His eyes began to moisten despite attempts to blink away his thoughts.

John stepped closer and gently placed his hands on the singer's shoulders. "Look, man, we can do it, but we can't do it without you. We know where you are now and if we could be with you we would. We can't. One more, Billy, okay?"

Billy sighed deeply and hesitated. He probed the face of each band member. "Okay, John . One more. I'll try."

Halfway through "Hurricane Season," the guitar player found himself staring down at the neck of his guitar as his fingers fumbled to find the right chords. He had forgotten the music to one of his own songs. His attempts at getting back on track were abruptly dispelled. He had tried, but he had failed. The rest of the band had stopped playing. The audience was silent. Billy looked contritely at each of The Wanderers. Each was staring at a spot just out from center stage. Billy followed their gaze.

It was Irena. She was wearing her cross and smiling. Billy smiled back. Time was frozen. He laid down his guitar and descended the stairs from the stage. He joined Irena and took her hands in his.

"You okay?"

"I've never been better. It's the two of us forever. I promise."

As the young couple clung to each other, the audience burst into extemporaneous cheers of approbation. To Billy, it was the best applause he had ever heard.

"Stay here, okay, Irena?" Billy shouted above the crowd. He was restored. He was complete.

"Sure, Billy, but why?"

"You'll see!"

Billy, bounded up the stairs two at a time until he reached the stage. He stopped suddenly and descended them in the same manner until he once again faced Irena.

"Irena, I forgot."

"Forgot what?"

"I love you."

"I love you too, Billy Emmerson!"

This time, Billy was even faster reaching the stage. Once positioned in front of his microphone, he gestured for silence. "Ladies and gentlemen, with the band's permission, I'd like to end this evening's concert by doing something a little different. I'm going to play a tune I wrote for someone very special."

Billy played "Irena's Song."

215

ISBN 1-41204193-7